M000194952

HADES

HADES

A JESS WILLIAMS WESTERN, NUMBER 49 IN THE SERIES

ROBERT J. THOMAS

This book is a work of fiction. Names, characters, places and incidents are either the product of the author's imagination or are used fictitiously. Any resemblance to actual events, locales, organizations or persons living or dead is entirely coincidental and beyond the intent of either the author and/or publisher. They are solely the imagination of the author and/or publisher and the imagination of events that may or may not possibly happen.

Copyright© 2016 by Robert J. Thomas

All rights reserved, including the right to reproduce this book or portions thereof in any form. No part of this text may be reproduced, transmitted, downloaded, decompiled, or stored into or introduced into any electronic or mechanical method without the written permission of the author and/or publisher. The scanning, uploading and distribution of this book via the Internet or via any other means without the written permission of the author and/or publisher is illegal and punishable by law.

A Jess Williams Novel.
Westerns. Revenge. Violence. Action. Adventure.
ISBN# 978-1-940108-37-7 – E-Book
AMAZON AISN# B01E727DAl (AMAZON ASSIGNED E-BOOK NUMBER)
ISBN: 1940108373
ISBN 13: 9781940108377

CHAPTER ONE

Wilhem Law and Epply Pearson sat at the table drinking from a bottle of rotgut whiskey. The bottle was almost empty and Law poured two more glasses, finishing it off. He tipped his head back and downed it in one gulp. He set the glass back down, saw the empty bottle and frowned at Pearson.

"I think we're out of whiskey," he slurred as he picked up the bottle and turned it upside down. A few drops fell on the table.

"I believe you're right, pardner," acknowledged Pearson as he closed his eyes tightly for a few seconds before opening them again, hoping the bottle would refill itself somehow. "Yep, it's still empty."

Law dug around in his pockets and found a few silver dollars. "I think I got enough for another bottle," he said as he held the coins close to his blurry eyes, closing one to see better.

"Then, go get us another bottle."

Law stood up and stumbled to the bar where the barkeep was talking to some other men. Law placed one silver dollar on the bar and smiled.

"Will this...buy me another bottle...of that stuff?" he stammered as he nodded at the empty bottle on the table.

ROBERT J. THOMAS

"Ain't you two had enough?" the barkeep asked. Law's head bobbed and swiveled around as he searched for the words in his muddled mind.

"Uh…no," he said as he pushed the silver dollar toward him.

The barkeep handed him another bottle and Law dropped it on the floor when he turned around and bumped into one of the other men standing at the bar. The bottle broke and splattered whiskey onto the men next to Law. The man he bumped into looked down at his pants and boots, shaking his head.

"You dang fool, you done spilt that stuff on my new boots," complained Lance "Lucky" Leyden. His friend standing next to him was looking at his own boots.

"He done got some on my boots too, Lucky," carped Dan Woodruff. Law squinted his eyes at Leyden.

"Why do they…call you…Lucky?"

"Because I'm lucky at everything I do," he answered smartly.

Law looked down at Leyden's whiskey-soaked boots and grinned drunkenly. "It don't look like you're…lucky right now," he said as he belched loudly.

Leyden waved his hands around in a futile attempt to move the sour stench in the air. "Mister, any luck you have is about to run out if you don't get the hell out of here right now," threatened Leyden.

"Why is that, Lucky?" drawled Law.

"Because I'm real lucky at pulling iron," he replied.

"So am I," said Law as he reached down with his left hand to feel for the butt of his pistol, but all he felt was his leg.

Leyden shook his head and leered at him. "Your iron is on your other leg."

Law reached down and felt the pistol. "Oh, there it is," he said, smiling drunkenly. "I must be turned around backward."

"Mister, I'm warning you, you'd best sit back down at that table with your friend," Leyden told him.

"But…but I need another bottle of whiskey."

"Why? So you can spill it on my boots again?" demanded Leyden, who was losing what little patience he had left.

"No, so I can drink it," slurred Law. Leyden picked up his glass of whiskey and threw it into Law's face. Law stepped back and licked the whiskey off his lips with his tongue and blinked his eyes repeatedly from the burning.

"How's that, you drunken fool?" growled Leyden.

"That's a fightin' offense," said Law.

Leyden thumbed his hammer strap off and stepped away from the bar. "Then reach for that leg cannon and see what it gets you next," he said.

Law took a few steps backward and jutted his face out at Leyden. "Let's see just how…lucky you really are."

The barkeep stepped back farther and looked at him. "Mister, why don't you sit down before he kills you?" warned the barkeep.

"Shut up and get ready to give me another bottle of whiskey," Law told him as he reached for his pistol, which didn't move since he'd forgotten to remove the hammer strap. He looked down at it and frowned as he tried to pull it out again.

"Uh-oh," he stammered as he looked up to see a gun barrel four feet from his face.

Leyden fired one slug that knocked Law's head backward and then his body followed as he fell onto the wooden floor. Leyden walked over to him and watched his feet twitch a few times. He replaced the spent shell in his pistol and turned to look at Pearson, who sat there stone still.

"You got something to say?" demanded Leyden.

"Nope," Pearson said as he looked at his dead friend on the floor with a pool of crimson red blood pooling under his head. Leyden holstered his pistol and walked back to the bar next to Woodruff. He looked at the barkeep, who was busy getting a bucket and mop.

"Barkeep, give me a towel so I can wipe off my new boots," growled Leyden. The barkeep threw him a towel and he bent over and started wiping off his boots. As he did, he looked between his slightly bowed legs and saw a figure standing just outside the batwings with a cut-down shotgun handle sticking over his right shoulder and a shrewd grin on his lips.

"Uh-oh," said Leyden as he dropped the towel on the floor.

"Hello, Lucky," said Jess, with a little emphasis on the word "Lucky," as he pushed through the batwing doors and moved to one side.

CHAPTER TWO

"I see you're up to the same old things," Jess told him as he leaned down slightly to view the dead body on the floor.

Leyden slowly stood up and turned toward Jess. "He spilt whiskey on my new boots," he said as he waved his hand at Law's body.

"And for that you shot him in the head?"

"He went for his pistol first."

Jess leaned over again and saw the hammer strap still tightly fastened on the hammer of the pistol. "His hammer strap is still on."

"That was his mistake. I wasn't about to tell the drunken fool."

"So, you just shot him?"

"Like I said, he went for his pistol first."

"Who the hell is that anyway?" asked Woodruff as he pointed at Jess.

Leyden lowered his head slightly. "That's Jess Williams, the bounty hunter," he muttered quietly. Woodruff stiffened and moved about five feet down the bar. Leyden glared at him.

"You desertin' me in my time of need?" he demanded of Woodruff.

"Hey, if that's Jess Williams, and he's lookin' for you, I don't want any part of it," declared Woodruff.

"Looks like your luck is running out," said Pearson from the table.

"You shut yer yap," Leyden scolded him.

"I think he's right, Lucky," said Jess as he pulled out the wanted poster and read it aloud. "Lance 'Lucky' Leyden, wanted dead or alive for the crimes of rape, train robbery, murder and being stupid," he said matter-of-factly before he threw the poster down on the nearest table.

"Does it really say stupid on there?" asked Leyden.

"Naw, I added that myself when I saw your horse outside."

"Well, I ain't stupid," refuted Leyden.

"Really?" asked Jess.

"That's what I said."

"You carved the word 'Lucky' on the side of your saddle on your horse so I knew you were in here."

"So what?"

"You carved it on both sides."

"I like the nickname."

"I'll tell them to put it on your grave marker," Jess told him.

"You ain't gonna arrest me?"

"You know I'm not."

"It says dead or alive on the poster."

"Yeah, but all I pay attention to is the first part where it says dead. Besides, there ain't no law in town here, so I'll have to drag your carcass to Avery to collect the bounty. I'm not listening to you complain all the way and try to run off at night."

"I promise to be quiet."

"Oh, I'm pretty sure I won't hear a peep out of you. Now, go ahead."

"Go ahead and what?" asked Leyden.

"See how lucky you are now," he told him as he nodded at Leyden's pistol.

He looked down at it and saw the hammer strap was still off. He inched his right hand down to the butt of it and wrapped his fingers around it. He smiled and slowly lifted it up far enough for the cylinder to spin and he thumbed the hammer back all the way. His smile got wider when he saw that Jess hadn't made a move for his pistol yet. His beady eyes narrowed as he jerked the pistol out, only to have the smile ripped from his face as he felt the slug punch a hole through his breastbone just below his chin.

His eyes crossed as he looked down at the bloody hole. His weakened fingers let the pistol drop to the floor. When it did, the hammer released and the slug hit Law's dead body, but he didn't move. Leyden fell sideways and Woodruff had to move a few feet farther down the bar. Jess glared at Woodruff, who unbuckled his gun belt and let it fall to the floor. He kicked it ten feet away and kept both of his hands in plain view.

"Smart man," Jess told him as he replaced his spent shell. "Who wants to make five dollars?" Pearson and Woodruff both raised their hands.

"Tie him down to his horse outside for me," Jess told them. They each grabbed a leg and hauled Leyden out of the saloon and busied themselves with strapping him down tightly.

Jess walked to the bar. "Any good whiskey back there?"

ROBERT J. THOMAS

"Didn't you read the sign above the door?" asked the barkeep. "It ain't called Rotgut Willie's for nothing." Jess sighed and picked up a pickled egg and popped it into his mouth.

"Those eggs are for the paying customers," the barkeep said nervously. Jess threw a silver dollar on the bar and picked up another egg.

"Do you want the whiskey?"

"No," Jess told him. "Give it to the man who was sitting at the table." Jess finished eating a third pickled egg when Pearson and Woodruff walked back in. Pearson was wearing Leyden's new boots. He smiled at Jess.

"You still get the same bounty with or without boots, right?" Jess nodded his head to say yes.

"Good, because I needed new boots," said Pearson as he saw the barkeep setting a bottle of rotgut on his table. "And more whiskey too?" He and Woodruff sat down at the table and Pearson poured two glasses of whiskey.

Pearson lifted the glass and looked down at his dead friend. "Sorry, pardner," he said.

Jess walked by their table on his way out. "It looks like it was your lucky day," he told Pearson before pushing through the batwing doors.

* * *

The short ride to the town of Avery from Appleton was a quiet one. Jess had tracked Leyden through several small towns and a few mining camps after leaving Reedy and Bodine at the split in the trail heading into Pelston. As he rode along the trail to Avery, he wondered if Malvern had gotten his California necktie yet. He smiled as he remembered the happy look on Lida Roddy's face as she went about the huge house cleaning every room and dusting every exotic-looking lamp.

Before riding into Avery, he sat atop his horse, Gray, and scanned the town with his spyglass. Nothing seemed out of the ordinary, so he put the spyglass away and nudged Gray into a slow walk toward the one end of the main street.

As he rode along the street, he saw two men slugging it out in front of a saloon. He stopped momentarily to scan the town thoroughly. He noticed an old white-haired man wearing a badge sitting in a rocking chair outside the jail watching the fight. He rode up to the jail and slid from the saddle. The badge on the man's shirt announced he was the town marshal. Groot Morrison looked up at Jess and then over at the dead body on the horse.

"Gotta wait until the fight is over," he said without standing up.

"Why don't you stop it?"

"Too much work. I just wait for one man to get knocked out and then I arrest the winner."

Jess turned to watch the fight. One man was much bigger and yet he was taking a beating from the smaller man, who kept dancing around and rushing in to pummel the big man again, only to rush out before the man could hit him back. The smaller man rushed in again and landed a left jab, followed by two hard left hooks that landed squarely on the big man's jaw. He staggered and fell face forward into the dusty street, out cold. Some of the men watching cheered and some jeered depending on whom they had bet money on. Morrison slowly stood up.

"Dang it, Ollie. I lost two dollars on that fight," he said to the winner.

"Sorry, you should have bet your money on me," Ollie said as he waved his hands around.

"Well, come on. You know I gotta lock you up for the night."

"Aw come on, Marshal," wailed Ollie as the barkeep threw him a towel so he could wipe the blood from the cut over his eye.

"You know the rule," argued Morrison.

Ollie collected his money from the spectators and walked to where the marshal waited. "You really going to lock me up again?" he asked.

"Either that or you pay the fine."

"How much is the fine?" asked Ollie as he dabbed his eye again. The marshal stuck his finger on his chin and looked as if he were calculating things in his head.

"I'd say the fine is exactly two dollars," he told Ollie.

"Two dollars," moaned Ollie. "Ain't that what you lost on the fight?"

The marshal's face took on a look of utter surprise. "As a matter of fact, that's exactly what I lost on the fight." He chuckled.

Ollie handed him two silver dollars and turned to look at Jess, who simply stood there watching. "You wanna fight me?" Ollie asked.

"I do my fighting with this," Jess told him as he tapped the butt of his pistol.

"If you change your mind, let me know," whispered Ollie. "You being new in town means we could tinker with the odds by telling everyone you're a trained pugilist."

"You looked like you knew what you were doing out there against that big man," said Jess as he saw two men helping him up.

"I do, but I told everyone in town that the big guy was a champion from out East." Ollie chuckled.

"Well, good luck to you, but I'll stick to bounty hunting," Jess told him. Ollie walked away and Morrison looked over at the dead body.

"So, who you got there?" he asked. Jess pulled out the wanted poster on Leyden and handed it to him.

Morrison read it and snorted. "He don't look lucky now. I can get you the money by tomorrow, but I always take a cut from it."

Jess put his hands on his hips and shifted his weight to his right foot. "And how much is your cut?"

"Fifty dollars," Morrison said briskly. "If I don't get my cut, it could take weeks or even months to fill out the proper paperwork."

"You know, you're worse than that fighter," Jess told him.

"Hey, a man's gotta eat. The town only pays me fifty a month and three squares a day at the local café."

"All right, fifty dollars is fair, I guess," agreed Jess. Morrison waved at an extremely short man in a tall black hat, who came running over.

"You need me to plant one, Marshal?" he asked.

"Yeah, put him in a shallow grave with no marker," he told the short man, who walked back and untied Leyden's horse from Jess's packhorse, Sharps. He started walking away and Jess turned back to the marshal.

"Don't you need to identify the body?" asked Jess.

"For fifty dollars, as far as I'm concerned, that's Lance 'Lucky' Leyden draped across that saddle," he said as he turned to go into his office.

Jess shook his head and watched the short man turn the corner. "I thought all undertakers were tall," he muttered.

Jess spotted the livery and headed for it. As he walked along the street, he went by a saloon on his left that was noisy and had several men outside drinking beer and laughing. He snapped his head to the right when he heard a door open and saw a young man walking out buckling his gun belt back on. A young woman was in the doorway blowing him a kiss. She locked eyes on Jess and wiggled her index finger at him. He smiled and tipped his hat at her, but kept walking. He heard the door close.

"Seems to be a happy town," he muttered to himself as he reached the livery.

CHAPTER THREE

Jess stabled his horses and headed over to one of the side streets where the livery worker told him he'd find a nice boardinghouse. Boran's Boardinghouse sat back from the street and had a garden planted in the front yard. It stood two stories tall and was painted meticulously with yellow paint on the walls and white trim on all the doors and windows. He opened the gate and walked up the path to the front porch where several rocking chairs were lined up. A heavyset man in a rumpled suit was sitting in one of them smoking a fat cigar. The man removed the cigar from his mouth as Jess took the two steps up to the porch.

"She won't let me smoke inside the place," said the man. "She's got a temper, so be careful, especially carrying all those rifles and guns."

"Thanks for the warning," Jess told him as he opened the screen door.

He walked in to find a middle-aged woman standing behind a small counter. Her eyes darted up above her spectacles first, followed immediately by her head bobbing up as she saw him standing there cradling his rifles with his saddlebags draped over his shoulders.

"Oh no, you're not staying here at my place, not with all those guns," she told him bluntly. "You march yourself right back out and get a room above one of the saloons in town."

"But they're usually too noisy to get much sleep," Jess told her.

"Then shoot someone if they're too loud. You sure got enough guns to do it."

"Listen, I'm no trouble. And I want your best room."

"Maybe you didn't hear me," She raised her voice. "I said you're not staying here."

"Listen, lady, I just hauled a body in from Appleton and I'm tired and hungry. How much do you charge for your best room?"

"Six dollars a night, but you're still not staying here."

"I'll pay you ten for the room for one night."

She stood up straight and eyeballed him for a long moment as she pursed her lips tightly and straightened her spectacles. "Make it twelve dollars and maybe I'll think about it."

"Are you related to the marshal?"

"Not that lazy scoundrel," she huffed. The screen door opened and Jess glanced behind him to see Ollie walking in. She stepped around the corner and saw the bandage over his right eye.

"Ollie Boran, have you been fighting again?" she demanded.

"Don't you start on me, Rosey," he grumbled. "Besides, I made fifteen dollars to help you run this place."

"You made fifteen dollars getting yourself beat up and I'm about to make fifteen dollars renting our best room for one night," she told him as she puffed out her chest.

"Really?" asked Ollie as he rubbed the cut above his eye.

"Yeah, really?" added Jess. "I thought we were talking twelve dollars a minute ago."

"I said I'd think about it and I decided to up it to fifteen dollars," she said.

"You can't charge the man fifteen dollars for one night," carped Ollie.

Jess looked back and forth between the two of them. "Really, I don't mind," he told them. "I just want to get a room. I'll pay the fifteen dollars."

Ollie stomped his foot on the floor. "What's next?" he asked her haughtily. "You gonna charge him twenty dollars if he eats his meals here?"

"Twenty dollars is a fair price for my cooking, Mr. Ollie Boran," she boasted as she jutted out her jaw.

"Hey, what happened to fifteen dollars?" asked Jess in a frustrated tone.

"You be quiet," she scolded him. "I'm having a conversation with my husband, who has obviously been hit in the head too many times."

"This is a conversation?" asked Jess.

"Stay out of this, bounty hunter," said Ollie.

"Hey, I'm just trying to get a room," he said as the veins in his neck starting to bulge.

Ollie stopped for a second as he looked at Jess's neck and then turned back to his wife again.

"Your cooking ain't that great that you could charge a man twenty-five dollars for a room," he yelled at her.

"Keep running that mouth of yours and see what you get for supper later," she hissed through clenched teeth.

"Why are you talking twenty-five dollars now?" Jess asked.

"Quit interrupting us," she scolded him. Jess moved to the counter, signed the register and placed twenty-five dollars on the counter as Ollie and Rosey continued to argue with one another. He turned to them and hollered.

"What room number is your best room?" They both shut up and swiveled their heads to look at him.

"Room five upstairs," she said calmly.

He removed the key for room five off the wall behind the counter and headed up the steps carrying all his things. Rosey smiled at the twenty-five dollars on the counter. She picked it up and shoved it into the pocket on her dress. She watched him walking up the steps.

"Are you joining us for supper?" she called up to him.

"I'm not sure I can afford it," he said, without turning around. She looked at his signature on the register and frowned.

"You signed your name *Frustrated*," she bellowed.

"That's because I am," he yelled back as he found his room and opened it.

He went inside, locked the door, put his things on one side of the bed and took a much-needed nap. Downstairs, Ollie and Rosey separated. Rosey went to the kitchen to start cooking for the guests and Ollie walked outside to pick some things from the garden.

Jess was stirred from his nap by the aroma of freshly baked bread. He opened his eyes and rubbed his face. He stood up, holstered his pistol and tucked the two short cut-down shotguns into the back of his holster. He put his back sling holding the large-bore on and unlocked the door. The aroma wafted through the entire upstairs. He heard a door open down the hallway and saw the man who had been

16

smoking a cigar on the front porch walk out of his room. He smiled at Jess as he ambled over to him.

"I told you she was a handful," he said in a quiet voice. "So, what'd you end up paying for the room?"

"Twenty-five dollars."

The man stiffened. "Dang, you could buy that room for that much."

"It was worth every penny not to have to listen to them a second longer."

"You going down for supper?"

"I'm almost afraid to," he said. "I think I already paid for meals, but I'm not certain of it."

"Listen, I stay here whenever I'm in this area. Just agree with everything she says and you have a better chance of not setting her off."

"Okay, I'll give it a try, but if she starts up again, I'm heading for the café I saw on Main Street." The two of them walked down the steps and to the kitchen. Rosey was stirring a pot of chicken stew and Ollie was slicing bread hot out of the oven.

"Afternoon, Mr. Cooper," she said as she smiled at the man in the suit. The smile vanished when she looked at Jess. "And a good afternoon to you, Mr. Frustrated."

"It smells wonderful," said Jess as politely as he could. Ollie shot Jess a warning look, shaking his head briskly when she wasn't looking.

"You two have a seat and supper will be served shortly," she said. "Help yourselves to the freshly baked bread on the table." Jess picked up a thick slice of the warm bread and slathered some butter on it as he watched Cooper do the same.

"Do you have a first name, Mr. Cooper?" Jess asked him. He nodded and put the knife down.

"Girard, Girard Cooper," he said before taking a large bite of the bread. "I'm a salesman of sorts. I sell pots and pans, kitchen items, things like that to boardinghouses, restaurants, cafés and even saloons around these here parts."

"Do you make any money at it?"

"Nowhere near the money you made on that dead man you brought in."

"You know about that?"

"The marshal told me about it." He took another bite of the bread. "One thousand dollars for one man is a whole heap of money."

Rosey stopped stirring and turned around. "You got paid one thousand dollars?" she asked. Jess nodded his head and smiled at her.

"I don't feel so bad about overcharging you now," she said curtly as she turned back around to the stove.

"It's a very nice room," he told her.

"Stop trying to get in my good graces, Mr. Frustrated," she said with a hint of sarcasm in her voice. Jess shut up and buttered another slice of bread.

Cooper looked at Ollie and the bandage over his eye. "I heard you made fifteen dollars on the fight today," he said.

"I would have made seventeen, 'cept I had to pay the marshal two dollars to stay out of jail for the night."

"You should have kept the two dollars and spent the night in jail," Rosey told him.

"I probably should have," he muttered under his breath.

"What did you say?" she demanded.

"I didn't say anything," he replied, smiling inwardly. Rosey dished out four platters of the stew. They sat down and everyone dug in. Rosey watched Jess eat, which made him slightly uncomfortable. Cooper noticed it and decided to break the awkward silence.

"So, Mr. Williams, what got you into the business of bounty hunting?" Cooper asked.

Jess swallowed his food and put his fork down. "My family was murdered when I was only fourteen," he said. "Once I killed the men responsible, it just seemed to come natural after that."

"There is nothing natural about killing men for money," scoffed Rosey.

"Someone has to do it," said Ollie. "That man he brought in today was a murderer, a rapist and a thief who parted other people from their money and families."

"Like you do when you fix the odds for fights?" blurted Rosey.

"Hey, you're only too happy to take the money I make every time I do it," he said. "Next time, let me keep the money."

Jess put his napkin down and slowly started to stand up. "Thanks for the meal. It was delicious," he said as he put his hat on, wanting to get out before the two got started again.

"Sit down and finish your supper," said Rosey. "We're done squabbling." Jess slowly sat back down as he looked to Cooper for unspoken advice. He smiled as if to say it was okay. When they finished eating, Jess stood up and donned his hat.

"If you gents want a drink at one of the saloons, I'm buying," Jess told Cooper and Ollie. They both nodded and stood up to leave.

"If you come home drunk or beat up from another fight, you'll be sleeping down in the lobby," Rosey warned Ollie. "And don't be messing with any of them dance hall girls."

"With what? You done took all my money," he protested as he walked out behind Jess and Cooper. When they got outside, Jess looked down the street at the saloon he had walked past earlier. The place was called Hunter's Inn and it was quite busy and noisy.

"Let's go to Hunter's," said Ollie. "I know the owner real good."

"It looks pretty busy," observed Cooper.

"It's always busy," said Ollie as he started walking toward it.

Ollie went in first, followed by Cooper with Jess bringing up the rear. As soon as they walked in, Jess scanned the room thoroughly. It was a mixture of cowpunchers, businessmen, farmers and a few men who looked like drifters. He saw Marshal Morrison sitting at a table with three other men wearing suits. Ollie made his way through the crowd until he found a spot at the bar. The owner, Bob Hunter, walked over to him.

"I made three dollars on that fight, Ollie," Hunter said smiling. "But a few of the locals are complaining about you claiming that the other man was a champion prize fighter."

"Hey, I let him cut me," he said as he pointed to the bandage over his eye.

"Even I saw you stick your head out for that one," cautioned Hunter. "A few of the men who were complaining are still in here and they've been drinking pretty heavy."

"Don't worry about it," scoffed Ollie. "Get us some whiskey."

Jess raised his hand and Hunter looked at him standing behind Ollie. "Make it your best whiskey," Jess told him.

"Sure thing, Mr. Williams," he said as he turned around and picked out a bottle from a shelf. Hunter poured three glasses of it. Ollie had taken one sip when a booming voice yelled out.

"Ollie, you owe me five dollars!" the deep gravelly voice claimed loudly as the noise started to ratchet down.

CHAPTER FOUR

Ollie, Jess and Cooper all turned around to see a tall, muscular man wearing overalls. He had a bushy beard and moustache and an angry look on his face.

Jess leaned over to Ollie. "Do you know that man?" he asked him.

"That's Newton Ludd," said Ollie. "He used to fight up in Missouri some years back."

"He doesn't look too happy," observed Jess.

"Actually, he looks like he's in a better mood than usual. Probably from the whiskey."

Jess looked at Ludd's angry eyes and frowned at Ollie. "He looks pretty mad to me."

Ollie raised his glass at Ludd and took a sip of the whiskey. "I won that fight fair and square," Ollie said.

"You said that man was a prize fighter from out East," argued Ludd. "I just had drinks with him and he says he never fought professionally in his life."

"He's just drunk and not thinking right after those last two left hooks I landed on the side of his head," proclaimed Ollie.

"Well, I still want my five dollars back that I lost betting on him," Ludd said angrily.

"You'll have to take the money from my wife, 'cause she done took all my winnings."

"I ain't messin' with that woman you're married to," said Ludd. "She'd take a skillet to my skull and I ain't one to hit any woman. If you don't give me my money back, I'll pound you into the ground and see what comes up next spring." The men in the place seemed to be getting excited now. Men were already exchanging money with one another for the new fight that seemed to be developing.

"Go on, Ollie. You can take him," hollered a voice from the crowd.

"Yeah, let's see another fight," said another voice.

Ollie looked at Jess. "Can you loan me ten dollars?" he asked as he rubbed the bandage over his eye.

"For what?"

"So I can place a bet on myself against Ludd," replied Ollie.

Jess looked the large burly man over again. "He looks to be six feet of solid muscle and you've already got a cut over your eye that'll open up as soon as you take a punch to your face," Jess lectured.

"I can take him," claimed Ollie.

"Okay, but you'll be sleeping in the lobby tonight," Jess told him as he handed him ten dollars.

"It's better than sleeping with that loud mouth I'm married to," he said as he took the money and held it in the air. "I'll bet ten dollars that I can knock Ludd out." The men became loud and boisterous as more money exchanged hands. Ludd pulled out some money and counted it, seeing he only had eight dollars left.

"I only have eight dollars left," hollered Ludd as he waved the money in the air. "Anyone want to loan me two dollars?"

Ollie smiled at Jess with amusement. "Lend him the two dollars," Ollie told him.

"Why should I lend him the money?" asked Jess.

"Why not?" said Ollie. "You paid twenty-five dollars for a six-dollar room."

"That was because I was worried it was going to thirty any second."

"Just give him two dollars," huffed Ollie. "You'll get back at least double after I knock him out." Jess let out a sigh, walked over and handed Ludd two dollars.

The owner of the place stood on top of the bar with a bucket hanging on a string around his neck and a piece of paper and pencil in his hands. He was taking bets, writing down names and figuring the odds for the fight. When no more bets were placed, Hunter climbed down from the bar and walked out to be the referee, which wasn't more than telling the two fighters to commence. Ollie removed his shirt and walked to the center of the room, where the men inside made a small circle. Jess found a spot at the bar where he could keep his back against the bar top. Ollie and Ludd met in the middle of the room and shook hands.

"I'm gonna pound on your head so long you'll have to look over your socks to see where you're going," threatened Ludd.

"That's mighty big talk for a man who can't move faster than a slug," cackled Ollie as he bounced up and down on his feet, moving his head back and forth. Hunter walked up between the two men and put a hand on each of their shoulders.

"Okay, men, no knives or objects used except for your own body parts," he said as he clapped his hands three times. "Let the fight begin!"

He darted out of the way as Ludd rushed at Ollie, who dove between his legs and came up behind him. He used his elbow to ram it against the back of Ludd's massive head. Ludd pitched forward into the crowd, but they pushed him back up. He turned to see Ollie dancing on his feet and smiling.

Ludd put his hands in the air and moved toward Ollie. He threw a wide right hand that Ollie avoided by moving his head back. As soon as the large fist swung an inch from his jaw, Ollie stepped in and threw two left hooks to Ludd's ribcage before moving behind him and using his right elbow to crack him in the back of his head. Ludd spun around and felt the back of his skull and saw the blood on his fingers. He rushed Ollie again and Ollie backed into the crowd, knowing they would shove him back toward Ludd. When they did, Ollie used his hands to grab the men behind him for support and stuck both of his feet in the air, locking his knees. Ludd slammed into his feet, knocking the wind from his lungs and almost knocking the entire crowd of men over.

Ollie somehow scrambled away from Ludd and ended up in the middle of the room, still bouncing on his feet. Ludd stayed bent over for a few seconds trying to refill his lungs. He stood up and slowly walked toward Ollie. He kept throwing wide right and left hooks that kept missing Ollie. Each time, Ollie darted in for a left or right hook to

Ludd's already tender ribs. Ludd rushed him like a bull and Ollie dove to the floor again, sliding past Ludd and coming up behind. He ran and jumped up and wrapped his legs around Ludd's neck and twisted him to the side, causing him to fall sideways onto the floor with Ollie's legs wrapped around his neck. Ludd used one hand to support himself while getting up as he used his other hand to claw at the spindly legs that kept tightening around his neck.

Ollie grabbed Ludd's hair and pulled back on his head until Ludd fell backward onto his back again with Ollie tightening his legs more and more as Ludd squirmed around trying to grab Ollie from behind him. Ollie's right hand let go of the hair and he began to pound Ludd on the side of his head repeatedly until blood started to trickle from the side of his head. Ludd's body began to move more and more slowly until he almost became lethargic from the loss of oxygen. Just as Ludd's eyes began to roll into the back of his head, Hunter rushed in and called the fight.

"It's over!" hollered Hunter as Ollie unwrapped his legs and crawled to his feet breathing heavily.

He raised his hands in the air and bowed at the crowd. Hunter helped Ludd sit up and handed him a bar towel to wipe the blood from his face. A few men walked over to Ludd and helped him to his feet. Hunter began handing out the winnings to the men who had bet on Ollie. The losers moaned and complained, but Hunter announced a free round of drinks to the losers as compensation. Ollie walked back over to Jess as he counted his winnings and handed Jess his earnings.

"See, you doubled your money, except for the two dollars you loaned Ludd," declared Ollie. "He's an ornery stubborn cur, but he's honest as they come and he'll pay you back."

"I'm not worried about the two dollars after seeing the beating he took," observed Jess.

"You almost have enough money for another night's stay at the boardinghouse," chuckled Cooper.

"At least I have a room," said Jess. "Ollie will be sleeping on the couch in the lobby tonight."

"Only if she finds out about the fight," he told them with a mischievous grin on his face. "So, which one of you will agree to tell her about it when we get back?"

CHAPTER FIVE

In the morning, Jess walked down the steps with all his things and found Ollie sleeping on the couch in the lobby. He heard noise in the kitchen and noticed Rosey peeking around the edge of the doorway to see him.

"Aren't you having breakfast with us this morning?" she asked.

"No, I'm heading out and plan to eat at the café on Main Street."

"You don't like my cooking?" she asked bluntly after putting her hands on her hips.

Ollie stirred on the couch and sat up. "Are you flapping your lips already this morning?" asked Ollie, holding his head in his hands. "Can't a man get some sleep?"

"Get your lazy behind up and pick me some things from the garden," she told him. Jess looked at Ollie and then at Rosey. Without saying a word, he darted for the door.

"You won't be getting any refund," she hollered at Jess.

"Don't want one," he said as Ollie followed him out into the front yard.

"Dang woman. I can't stand being married to her, but I got nowhere else to go," he carped. "She owns the place lock, stock and barrel."

"Go find an old abandoned mine shack."

"I ain't got a horse."

"Go buy one," said Jess. "You won plenty of money last night." Ollie reached into his pockets and they were empty.

"Dang it, she already emptied my pockets while I was sleeping," he sighed. "Let me go along with you. We can hunt down someone and split the bounty money. Then I could live on my own in some other town."

"Do you even have a rifle?"

"Naw, don't own any guns, but you've got plenty of them, plus I saw you had a packhorse I could ride."

Jess stood there feeling a little sorry for him, but the thought of taking on someone who knew nothing about the business of hunting men made him frown and shake his head. He turned to see Rosey standing in the doorway watching them, one hand on her hip, the other holding a heavy skillet.

"Sorry, Ollie. Sometimes a man just has to save himself," Jess told him as he walked out the gate and closed it, leaving him standing there like a lost child.

"Quit standing there and start digging me some taters from the garden in the back," ordered Rosey as she raised the skillet up to her shoulder.

Ollie's shoulders slumped as he headed around to the back of the boardinghouse. Jess walked to the livery on Main Street and saddled his horses. He walked them over to a general store to stock up on supplies. When he finished packing his saddlebags, he saw the marshal moving his way with an envelope in his hand. Jess circled around his horses to meet him.

"It's all in there, except the hundred you agreed to let me keep," said Morrison chuckling.

"I thought we agreed on fifty dollars."

"Really? I guess I didn't remember it that way."

"Are you related to the woman who owns the boardinghouse?"

"Why do you ask?"

"She charged me twenty-five dollars for a six-dollar room."

"I taught her that trick." He chuckled again. "That old bat is my sister."

"She denied being related to you."

"Good. I try to avoid her as much as I can," he said. "The only reason I lock Ollie up after a fight is because she makes me do it. I have to split the fine with her."

"Ole Ollie doesn't stand a chance," said Jess as he shook his head.

"No, he sure don't," agreed Morrison.

"Why'd he marry her?"

"Might have had something to do with the fact that I was holding a shotgun to his back."

"You made him marry her?"

"It was the only way to get her off my behind," said Morrison. "When our mother died, she left the deed to the boardinghouse to her and I got nothing. Ollie came through town back then and she took a liking to him. Things were fine for a few years, but when the luster rubbed off, she started nagging him so bad he threatened to leave her. I got the preacher and my shotgun and made them marry. I kind of regret it some now, seeing how Ollie has to live."

"That's why he wanted to come with me," said Jess.

"You don't want to take him with you."

"I wasn't planning on it," he said. "I told him no and left him back at the boardinghouse."

"So, where are you off to now?" asked Morrison. Jess grinned when he took out the wanted poster on Lowe Rogan and showed it to him.

"You're going after Lowe Rogan?" he asked nervously.

"Yeah, I've heard he hangs around a town called Hades, but I don't see it on any map I have of Texas," Jess told him.

"That's because no one wants anyone to know where that hellhole of a town is," said Morrison as he handed the wanted poster back to Jess.

"Do you know where it is?"

"You don't want to go there."

"I do if that's where Rogan is."

"Go looking for someone else, but don't go to Hades looking for Rogan," he said with worry evident on his face.

"Why not?"

"That town rose straight up from the depths of hell," he told him as an icy shiver crawled up his spine. "If you go there and find Rogan, if you survive that is, don't bring his body back here for the bounty."

"Not even if I give you ten percent of it?"

"You could give me the entire thousand dollars and I still wouldn't take it," he said. "If you bring anyone from that town here, hell will surely follow you. That town is filled with ghosts and demons."

"I don't believe in ghosts, and demons are the thoughts that live in a bad man, but he is still a man who will bleed from a bullet."

"You're not hearing me," scolded Morrison. "If you go there, don't come back here. I mean that."

"Thanks for the warning, Marshal, but I'm heading there anyway, so you might as well point me in the right direction."

"No, I won't do it," he said as he turned and walked away.

Jess watched him and wondered why he was so scared that he wouldn't even tell him which direction to ride in. He saw Cooper walking out of a saloon carrying a suitcase. He made his way toward him and when Cooper noticed, he waved and smiled. Jess walked up to him and looked at the suitcase.

"Oh, I have samples inside it," explained Cooper. "I've been trying to make a few sales this morning. You missed a very good breakfast. You should have joined us since you ended up paying so much for your room."

"I had to get away from those two," he said grinning knowingly. "Anyway, can you tell me where the town of Hades is?" The color drained from Cooper's face as he stood there stone still and silent for the longest time.

"Cooper?" Jess asked him. "Are you okay?"

Cooper shook his head slowly. "You don't want to go there," he said in a quiet voice as if he were afraid someone could hear him.

"That's what the marshal said."

"You should listen to him."

"Why is everyone afraid to even tell me where this town is?"

Cooper set his suitcase down and removed his suit jacket. He put the jacket over his suitcase and rolled the sleeves on his shirt up to his elbows. He showed the inside of his forearms to him. Jess leaned over and saw the scars that looked like they were made to look like symbols of some sort. What really interested him was that both arms had the same exact symbols in the exact same places on his forearms.

"Who did that to you?"

"I have no idea, except that when I visited Hades, I went to sleep the first night and woke up with these on my arms. I got myself out of that hell-hole as soon as I could that morning. When I rode out, there were two heads stuck on poles on the trail leaving town. There were two piles of bones left on the ground below the heads. They weren't bloody and looked like they had been boiled. I almost rode my horse to death getting away from there. I swear I could feel the flames of hell following me." Cooper quickly rolled his sleeves down and buttoned them. He put his suit jacket back on.

"I know you're good with them guns of yours, but that's not a town you want to visit," he said frankly.

"Can you at least tell me which direction it is?"

"You won't change your mind?"

"No."

"It's straight south of here and a good three-day ride through some of the roughest territory I've ever seen. There probably ain't an honest soul left in that town. I think it's been damned since it rose straight up from hell. They should have called it purgatory, because all the worst men and demons live there on their way to hell."

"Thanks," said Jess.

"No, don't thank me for telling you about it," said Cooper as he picked up his suitcase and walked away. Jess stood there looking over at Morrison rocking in his chair outside of his jail. He was watching Jess and shaking his head slowly.

"They've got me wondering about it now," Jess whispered to himself.

CHAPTER SIX

Jess rode out of Avery along a trail leading south. Way off in the distance he could see mountainous terrain. He followed the trail and toward the end of the first day, it changed from a clear well-used trail to one of rough, rocky terrain where another trail veered off to the east. He stopped at the split and looked around. It looked as if the trail continuing south hadn't been used by many people.

He continued on until an hour before dark. He made camp, making sure he placed as many cans and strings as possible around his perimeter. He ate jerky and hardtack, not wanting to start a fire that late in the day. He slept lightly that night, waking often to any sounds that he would normally ignore. Wolves howled in the night.

In the morning, he made a large breakfast and as he was ready to dig in, he heard the clomping of a horse's hooves on the rocky trail. He slid the large-bore out of his back sling as he stood up and turned. The horse slowly came into view as it rode over a rise in the trail.

Jess stiffened at the sight of a headless rider who seemed to bob and weave in the saddle. He raised the shotgun and watched as the horse walked closer to him. He saw all the ropes that were holding the body in the saddle. The horse stopped in front of Jess. He walked to it and rubbed its forehead.

"Easy, boy," he whispered as he moved to the side of the horse to see the dead body.

Someone had stuck a plank board under the man's shirt to keep his back stiff. Ropes were tied around his body tightly. Jess took the reins of the horse and tied them to a nearby bush. Then he put his large-bore back into his back sling and started cutting the ropes from the body until it eventually fell off the other side of the horse. Jess walked around to the body and went through the pockets. He found no money, but there was a folded piece of paper inside the front pocket of the man's bloodied shirt. He unfolded the paper and looked at it. The note was written in blood and it said: *The demons in Hades took my head*. He stuck the note into his pocket and stood up.

"Someone really doesn't want anyone to go to that town," he whispered to himself. He looked down at the headless corpse.

"I don't suppose you want half of my breakfast?" he asked before looking up at the vultures soaring high in the sky. "It looks like you'll be the next meal after I leave though."

He ate his meal, drank some coffee and unsaddled the dead man's horse. He slapped it on the rump and the horse took off and stopped at the first patch of grass it found. Jess cleaned up and headed along the rough trail again. He rode all day, eating lunch in the saddle. On the third day, he was closer to the mountainous area, but he still couldn't see any town. After the noon hour, he decided to ride up a small hill to see what he could see. When he reached the top, he pulled his spyglass out and scanned the area ahead. He almost went by it, but he stopped and focused on one building that he could see behind some hills.

"Gotta get a little closer," he whispered to himself.

He rode down the hill and along the trail, which was strewn with rocks and small bushes. As he got closer, he saw some vultures feasting on what looked like a dead body. The large birds soared in the air as he got closer and disturbed them. He looked down at the naked body. It had been chewed up fairly well, but he could see the remnants of a distinct arrow that had been carved into the man's chest. The arrow pointed north toward Avery. He pulled out some beef jerky, took a large bite of it and chewed as he kept looking back and forth between the dead body and the building he saw behind the hill. He patted Gray on his neck.

"I think we have a little scouting to do before we try to ride into that hell-hole," he told Gray, who snorted and shook his head.

He had been riding for a few minutes when he saw a rider way off in the distance turn the corner of the building he had seen. Whoever the rider was, he was approaching at a moderate pace. Jess reined up his horses, slipped his hammer strap off and slid his Winchester out. He racked a shell into it and waited for the rider to reach him. The rider slowed his horse to a walk and rode up to where Jess waited. The man had his hand on the butt of his pistol. The fact that his hammer strap was off was not lost on Jess. The man wore a red-and-white checkered shirt, black denims and a black Stetson that had seen better days.

"Are you plannin' to ride into Hades?" the man asked nervously after seeing the rifle resting on Jess's thigh, the hammer already eared back.

"I was thinking on it," Jess told him.

"Mister, you'll find nothing but trouble there."

"Maybe I'm looking for trouble."

"Ain't many honest people left in that town."

"And are you one of them?"

"One of who?"

"The honest ones you mentioned."

"Well, yeah, I was just passing through, but the bad ones in that town ran me out," he said as he fidgeted in the saddle.

"Then how do you explain the fact that I have a wanted poster with your face on it in my front pocket?" The man stiffened at the accusation and shook his head.

"You a bounty hunter?"

"Good guess. On the first try too."

"Well, that can't be true," he said pompously. "I ain't wanted by the law."

"The law says different."

"Show me the wanted poster."

"Why? So you can take advantage of the situation when I reach inside my pocket?"

"No, because I say I ain't wanted and you need to prove to me that I am or let me go."

"I don't have to prove anything to you," Jess told him. "I only have to show the wanted poster to the law when I turn you in for the bounty. If I've got the wrong man, I go to prison; but I ain't got the wrong man."

The man nervously turned his head toward the town and then back to Jess.

"How much am I worth?"

"Five hundred dollars."

"If we start shootin' it out, they'll come out to see what it was about," he said as if it were a warning.

"Who will come out?"

"There's close to a dozen cold-blooded killers in that godforsaken town."

"I heard it was full of demons and devils."

"I can't argue with that. Some strange things happen in that town."

"Like what?"

"People wake up with scars on their arms and some of them don't wake up at all, if you get my drift. Yesterday, they hauled out one of the few townsfolk living in town and burned her on a wooden cross claiming she was a witch or something like that. That's why I left today. I admit, I killed a man as a revenge killing, but I'm not a cold-blooded murderer. The man killed my younger brother and he wasn't even armed at the time. The fact that the man I killed happened to be the brother of the town marshal is the only reason I have that bounty on my head."

Jess studied the man for a few moments, watching his eyes closely. "I'm also looking for a man by the name of Lowe Rogan. Did you see him in town?"

"There is a man there they call Lowe, but they never said his last name. He's the one who threw the match on the fire to burn that poor woman to death."

"Could you identify him if I showed you a wanted poster with his likeness on it?"

"Yeah, I probably could."

"Then put that hammer strap back on." The man put his hammer strap on and Jess placed the rifle across his legs. He pulled out the wanted poster on Lowe Rogan and showed it to the man.

He quickly nodded his head. "Yeah, he's in town now. He's the one who set fire to that woman I told you about."

He handed the poster back to Jess with an expectant look. "So now what?" he asked.

Jess pulled out the wanted poster on the man and showed it to him as he read it aloud. "Guy Taylor, wanted dead or alive for five hundred dollars for a revenge killing," said Jess as he handed it to Taylor, who looked at it and sighed.

"Just who the hell are you anyway?" asked Taylor.

"Jess Williams."

The man sat straight up as the name sank in. "You're the bounty hunter who always brings his man in dead," he said with a look of worry. "But like I said, if you shoot me, they'll come out here and kill you."

Jess sat there staring at Taylor. He believed his version of the story on the shooting, plus Taylor was right. Any gunshots would bring the killers out. Even with his two horses, he'd never escape over the rough terrain.

Jess smiled at him. "Well, Guy Taylor, it looks like this is your lucky day," Jess said as he nodded at the trail behind them. "Get on out and pray I don't see any new wanted posters on you. If I do, I'll be coming for you again and it won't be your lucky day when I do."

"Thanks, Mr. Williams. You won't regret this, I promise you," he said with obvious relief on his face.

He kicked his horse into a slow gallop. Jess turned his horse and watched until Taylor was out of sight. He turned back to the building in town and pulled his spyglass out, looking at it again. The building was painted a dark red, like the color of drying blood.

"Interesting," he muttered to himself as he turned his horses toward the backside of the hill that hid most of the town they called Hades.

CHAPTER SEVEN

The main street of Hades appeared desolate. Not one soul was outside and it was after the noon hour. Nothing seemed to move, not even the two mongrel dogs that hid under the boardwalk. Even they were afraid to come out. A broken-down wagon stood in the middle of the street, one of the wheels partially off and leaning. No horse was hitched to it. Tumbleweeds occasionally wandered through, bumping into the edge of the boardwalk and making their eerie way out the other side of town. The street was dusty and the wind picked up dirt and swirled it around into a dust devil.

The town had one saloon on Main Street. The name was faded now. The sun, wind and rain had long ago washed the hand-painted letters away. The batwing doors that used to swing years ago were now completely gone. Only a doorway leading into the place remained. Lester Roper stood in the doorway, sipping on whiskey as his dark inset eyes keenly scanned the street.

"What are you looking at?" asked his brother, Elam, from inside the saloon. Lester slowly moved his head around to see his brother playing a card game by himself.

"Just checking to see if that Taylor feller was still hanging around," he told Elam.

"I told you, he high-tailed it out of here. He started worrying we'd make an example out of him. He didn't want to find his head on a stick on one of the trails leading into this hell-hole." Lester laughed a low evil laugh, more to himself than to his brother.

"Yeah, I suppose he did after we burned that woman on the cross out there," he said as he looked at the burned remains of their dastardly deed barely hanging from the wooden cross.

There were several other men in the saloon. Most of them stayed silent. All of them were wanted men, hiding from the law. They knew no lawman would come there looking for them, except maybe a United States Marshal or a Texas Ranger, but there weren't many of those around and not many people even knew of the town's existence anymore. Anyone who had visited the town and lived never returned and never talked about it. There were only about a dozen locals left who still called it home, but they were afraid to attempt to leave for fear they'd end up a pile of bones on one of the trails leading into Hades.

Blake Archer, the owner and barkeep of the saloon, stood behind the bar, wiping down glasses. Not because they were dirty, but because he needed something to do to pass the time. He had dodged the law for years until he finally settled down here when things were normal. He sometimes laughed at the irony of his situation. He had gone straight ten years ago and opened the saloon, only to have the town taken over by some of the worst killers and thugs out there. His dream of living a normal life had long ago faded, although he was better equipped to deal with the killers and thugs, since he had been one of them before.

Lester stayed in the doorway for a while, watching one of the dogs lying under the boardwalk across the street from him. The dog scratched the side of its head with its rear paw and then settled back down on the ground. Some movement to his left caught his attention and when his eyes slowly moved in that direction, he saw two of the local townsfolk walking to the burned remains of the woman still tied to the cross in the middle of the street. They carried blankets with them, obviously intent on burying the remains. Lester, in his depraved mind, allowed the two men to actually begin to reach for the woman's corpse before he called out to them.

"What the hell do you think you're doing?" he hollered. The men froze.

"We just thought it was okay to finally bury her proper," one of them said timidly, afraid to look directly at Lester.

"You thought that, did you?" asked Lester as he rolled the chaw to the other side of his mouth with his tongue.

"Yeah," said the other man. Lester stepped out of the doorway and into the light. His mean eyes drilled into the two men as he spat some brown liquid onto the boardwalk.

"Who told you that either of you could think?" he demanded. Both men looked down at the ground, still afraid to look up at him.

"I asked you both a question and I expect an answer," growled Lester as his right hand rested on the butt of his pistol.

"We didn't mean nothing by it," answered one man. "I used to be the preacher in town."

"So, you're a preacher?" queried Lester.

"I am."

"Will you pray for my soul?" asked Lester.

The preacher finally looked up at him. "I'm not sure it would help you much," he replied.

Lester's eyes narrowed at the man as anger danced in his dark eyes. "You'll either agree to pray for my soul down here or I'll send you upstairs so you can talk to the man personally about it," he said as he thumbed the hammer on his Colt back, drew the pistol out of his holster and held it down by his leg.

"All right, I'll pray for your soul as best I can," he said as he quickly made the sign of the cross.

"That's what I thought," said Lester as he released the hammer and holstered his pistol. "Now, go ahead and clean up that mess and put me up another wooden cross in case I feel like burning another one of your devout followers."

The preacher and the other man began the ugly process of picking up the remains of the body and putting them in the blankets. When they got most of it, they wrapped the blankets up and started hauling them to the local cemetery.

The preacher looked at the other man. "I'll pray for his soul all right," he muttered softly. "I'll pray someone comes to take it and send it straight to hell."

Inside the saloon, Lowe Rogan sat with two other men playing a game of poker, using peanuts as money. He threw his hand on the table and poured himself another shot of whiskey.

"I gotta get the hell out of here pretty soon," he said.

Elam heard him and looked over in his direction. "You can do the next whiskey run," said Elam. "We're runnin' low."

"I can take Carmichael here with me," said Rogan. "He can drive the wagon to Chilton."

Carmichael looked up from his cards. "Why do I have to drive the wagon?" he complained.

"Because I said so," said Rogan.

Carmichael sighed and smiled at his cards. He had a full house. He threw them down on the table and grinned, exposing his yellow stained teeth. "Looks like I win," he said.

Rogan shook his head at him. "All you're winning is peanuts, you idiot," he said.

"I like peanuts," he said as he cracked one open and stuck the nut into his mouth. "I'll go and hitch the wagon up while you get the money for the whiskey.

* * *

After leaving Taylor on the trail, Jess slowly worked his way up the hill that overlooked Hades. When he reached the top, he climbed out of the saddle and scanned the town below through his spyglass. Every building had been painted the same dark red color. He saw two men at the end of town digging a grave at the local cemetery. He didn't see a pine box or a body, just two blankets sitting near the men digging.

He watched the doorway to the saloon, but Lester was sitting inside now, so he didn't see any movement until two men walked out. He recognized one of the men as Lowe Rogan. They walked to the livery. A while later, Rogan came out riding a horse while the other man was in a small wagon being pulled by a mule. They rode down Main Street and headed along a trail heading east.

"Well, wherever you're going, I'm going," Jess muttered to himself as he backed away from the top of the hill.

He climbed up on Gray and made his way down the rocky hillside. He rode over the terrain where there was no trail, moving slowly so his horses didn't throw a shoe or get hurt by the rocky ground. He eventually made his way to the trail the wagon and Rogan had been on and saw the fresh tracks.

He could see the dust trail way ahead of him. He turned in the saddle to see the town off in the distance. He sat in the saddle for a moment, determining whether or not to go into the town or follow Rogan. Even though he hadn't see them all, he knew there had to be plenty of cold-blooded killers in Hades, but his best chance of getting them all was to divide and conquer them at his pace. He nudged Gray into a slow cantor in the direction Rogan and the wagon had gone. He didn't know who the other man was, but there was a good chance he was wanted by the law. He followed along slowly, wanting to keep a good distance between them, at least for now.

CHAPTER EIGHT

When Rogan and Carmichael reached the sleepy town of Chilton, Texas, they rode to the general store and reined in. Any of the locals who saw them quickly looked away, including the town marshal. Carmichael climbed down from the wagon and looked up at Rogan.

"I'll buy what I can in the store, but you'll have to go to the saloon and buy a few cases of whiskey," he told Rogan, who handed him some money for the supplies in the store as he looked over at the saloon.

"As soon as you load the wagon, drive it over to the saloon," Rogan told him.

"Okay," he said as he walked up the steps and inside.

Rogan took his horse to the saloon and dismounted. He looked around town before removing his hammer strap and walking inside. As soon as he pushed through the batwing doors, every set of eyes in the place fell on him for a few seconds. He made his way to the bar, where the barkeep was talking to another man.

"Whiskey," he told the barkeep, who poured him a shot of rotgut.

"Just passin' through?" queried the barkeep.

"Yeah, and I need a few cases of whiskey to take with me."

"You got the money?" asked the barkeep. Rogan placed some bills on the bar. The barkeep smiled as he took the money.

"I'll get it for you," he said as he turned around and headed for his storage room. He carried out two cases, followed by two gallon jugs filled with whiskey that hadn't been cut with any turpentine or varnish.

"These two jugs are the good stuff," he said. Rogan nodded as Carmichael drove the wagon up in front of the saloon. He jumped out of the seat and headed inside.

Jess watched Carmichael turn the wagon around in the street and ride to the saloon from the end of the street where he was standing next to a building. As soon as Carmichael was inside, Jess walked along the boardwalk until he was close to the saloon. He ducked between two buildings and waited.

He heard growling and looked down under the boardwalk where he saw a large lanky dog on the ground close to where he stood. The dog showed its teeth as another low guttural growl emanated from it. Jess reached inside his back pocket, pulled out a piece of jerky and threw it to the dog. It took a sniff, picked it up with its teeth and began chewing on it. Jess watched the dog for a few seconds until he heard the swinging doors creaking open. He looked up to see Rogan and the other man walking out, each carrying a case of whiskey. He quickly stepped out from the buildings with his hammer strap off.

"Who's your friend, Rogan?" he asked. Rogan and Carmichael both stood stone still as they looked over at him.

"Who the hell are you?" asked Rogan.

"I'm the man who's going to collect one thousand dollars on your head."

"How do you know I'm wanted by the law?"

"I have the wanted poster in my front pocket."

"You must have the wrong man," Rogan said as he slowly lowered the case of whiskey to the boardwalk.

"I don't think so," argued Jess. "I just need to know if your friend is wanted too."

"Carmichael is a man of the cloth," lied Rogan.

"Not too many preachers around who carry a Navy Colt tied down tight and low like that," said Jess as he nodded at Carmichael's pistol.

"This is dangerous territory," grinned Rogan as he slowly stood up and inched his hand closer to the butt of his pistol.

"I reckon it is," agreed Jess. "So, were you planning on taking the whiskey back to Hades?" Carmichael and Rogan exchanged anxious looks at the mention of their hideout.

"I don't know anything about Hades except for the fact that I suspect I'll see it one day," replied Rogan cagily.

"Maybe sooner than you think," suggested Jess as he smiled unnervingly at the two men. Carmichael slowly lowered his case of whiskey to the boardwalk and stood back up, moving his right hand close to the butt of his pistol.

"Mister, I don't know who the hell you are and I don't give two shits about what you want, but you'd better back away and ride out while you still can," he said through mean, angry eyes as his lips curled up into an ugly sneer.

"And if I don't, are you gonna pray for me, Preacher?" Jess asked with a hint of sarcasm.

"You'd best start prayin' for yourself," warned Carmichael.

Jess smiled at Carmichael when he spoke. "I know Rogan's worth a thousand, but I'm guessing you're worth something too."

"I'm warning you, Mister, you'd best leave this alone," said Carmichael as his hand crept closer to the butt of his pistol.

Jess cocked his head slightly and grinned that slightly evil grin. "Move that hand another gnat's ass and you'll be headed for Hades with Rogan. And I'm not talking about the town you rode out of earlier," he warned him.

Carmichael's face slowly scrunched up into an evil sneer before he jerked for his pistol. Rogan followed a split second later, which was all the time it took for Jess to slick his pistol out and fire two shots in the blink of an eye.

The first slug punched straight through Rogan's chest, knocking him backward and onto his back, his pistol flying up in the air, landing behind him a good ten feet. The second slug tore a bloody hole through Carmichael's throat, causing him to drop his cocked pistol on the boardwalk as both his hands grabbed his throat in an attempt to slow the flow of blood gushing out. Carmichael gave Jess an astonished look as his eyes rolled up into the back of his head. He fell forward until he landed on the case of whiskey bottles. At first, he looked stiff, but as the life drained from his body, he slowly slumped over whiskey.

Jess walked up to the other case of whiskey and looked down at Rogan, who was holding his chest with both hands, trying to stem the flow of blood. Rogan's eyes were looking up at the overhang, but they slowly fell on Jess as he stepped over the whiskey. Jess looked at Rogan, tilting his head back and forth as he did.

"Just who the hell are you, Mister?" coughed Rogan.

"Jess Williams."

"I don't think I know that name."

"Don't matter much now."

"I'm gonna die, ain't I?"

"I figure with the way you're bleeding, you got about three minutes."

"It burns like hellfire."

"I imagine it does."

"Can you spare a bullet for a dead man?"

"You mean, can I end your suffering?"

"Would you?"

"Depends."

"On what?"

"Who's left back in that town you rode out of?"

"I don't know them all," he said as he coughed up some lung blood. "Elam and Lester Roper are the leaders of the pack. Saul Rivard and Jacob Powell are two more I know of who are there. I don't know the others."

"How many of the townsfolk have they killed so far?"

"Three or four, I think," he said as he wheezed and gurgled. "Can I get that bullet now?" His eyes begged for the suffering to be over.

Jess looked down at him with no pity. "I heard you were the one who set that woman ablaze. Is that true?"

Rogan slowly nodded his head. "Yeah, I did it," he admitted. "You should have seen the look on her face when that lamp oil caught fire."

"I only wish I could kill you twice," Jess told him as he aimed at his forehead and put a slug between his eyes.

"Are you out of your mind!" hollered a voice coming from a man running toward him wearing a badge on his shirt and a frightened look on his face.

CHAPTER NINE

As the man got closer, Jess saw he was the town marshal. He was short and skinny with a balding head. He stopped at the edge of the boardwalk and looked at the two dead men lying on it.

"That man is wanted for one thousand dollars," Jess informed him.

The marshal was shaking his head back and forth slowly. "I know that," he barked. "And now that you've gone and killed him, the Roper brothers will want revenge. And, when they want revenge, they come and kill someone and that someone might be me."

"You know about all this?"

"Yeah, I know all about the town of Hades and the killers who hide there," he replied awkwardly. "As long as they don't bother us, we don't bother them."

"They're killers and thieves."

"So what?" he said as he waved his arms around haphazardly. "There are killers and thieves all over this damn state. No one can round them all up because there ain't enough law. So I leave those men in Hades alone."

"And what if they decide to come and visit your town and stay a while?"

"That's exactly what I'm trying to avoid, but now you done gone and killed two of them," he wailed.

Jess pulled the wanted poster on Rogan out of his pocket and held it out for the marshal to read. "I expect to be paid my bounty money and if you have a wanted poster on the other man, I expect to be paid for him too," Jess told him bluntly.

"I know exactly who he is. That's Arron Carmichael and he's worth three thousand dollars. He's also got a brother who will be looking for the man who killed him."

"Then I reckon you owe me four thousand dollars in total."

"I don't think you're listening to me," carped the marshal.

Jess shot him a pitiless glance before looking around at all the people gathering around and listening. "Why don't you get the undertaker to come for the bodies and let's go to your office to discuss this."

The marshal began to say something, but clamped his jaw shut and turned around and headed to the jail. Jess saw a tall man wearing a black stovepipe hat heading toward the bodies. He replaced the spent shells in his pistol and holstered it before heading across the street to the jail. When he walked in, the marshal was sitting behind his desk holding his head in his hands. A nameplate on the desk had the name Marshal Marvin Schneider on it. Jess sat down in the chair across from him and threw the wanted poster on Rogan on his desk.

"How long before I collect my money?" Jess asked Schneider, who slowly looked up at him.

"Money?" he asked. "You want your money?"

"Yeah, that's how this works. The law puts a bounty on a bad man's head, I find him and put him down and the law pays me for my services."

"Well I'm worried about my town right now, thanks to you," complained Schneider.

"You have a badge and a gun."

"And what's that supposed to mean?"

"You're sworn to uphold the law and protect the people in this town."

"I'm only one man and the Ropers are the meanest men I know."

"Then deputize every man in town, issue them all rifles and have them stand guard from the rooftops if necessary."

"It's not just the Ropers," he said edgily.

"Then what else is it?"

"That town is cursed. They've got witches and demons living there."

"That's not true."

"Yes it is. They burned a witch on a wooden cross in the middle of town last year."

"And they burned another woman the same way the other day, but she wasn't a witch, just an innocent woman who was killed in the worst way to make you think the town is cursed."

"They burned another witch?"

"No, you idiot, they burned another woman."

"So, you don't believe the town is cursed?"

"Yeah, with the Roper brothers and a bunch of killers that no one seems to want to deal with."

"No one will go to that town except for the occasional drifter or salesman who come across it," said Schneider. "And most of them never come back out."

"Marshal, I don't know what else to tell you, but I'm expecting to get paid my bounty money."

"If the Ropers find out I paid you for killing two of their men, they'll come and hang me from the nearest tree," he declared.

"And if you don't pay me my money, they'll find you locked behind bars in your own jail cell," threatened Jess.

"You've got no authority to do that."

"You might be surprised to find out what authority I have," he told him as he lost all patience over the matter. "Tomorrow morning I get paid or you get locked up until I do."

Schneider narrowed his eyes and glared at him. Then he took out a slip of paper from his desk and grudgingly shoved it across to him. "Sign your name on that last line," he told Jess. He signed it and when Schneider read the name, he looked up from the form with surprise splattered across his face.

"You...you're Jess Williams?" he asked.

"That's correct."

"Jess Williams...the bounty hunter?"

"Yes."

"I'll have your money ready for you in the morning," he said as he stared at the signature on the form.

"I'm glad we finally came to an understanding," Jess said as he stood up.

Schneider kept staring at him. "So, are you going to Hades?" asked Schneider.

Jess stopped at the doorway and turned to give the marshal a firm look. "Let's just say that you should notify the bank that you'll be paying out some more bounty money in the very near future," he said before he walked out and down to where he had left his horses.

"Aw, hell," moaned Schneider as he hung his head and shook it.

Jess found his horses right where he had left them. He walked them along the street. When he went past the saloon, the two cases of whiskey and the wagon were gone and a man was mopping the blood off the boardwalk. A bottle of whiskey was on the boardwalk close to the man, obviously payment for his grisly labor.

He found the livery and stabled his horses, carrying his things to the saloon since he hadn't seen any boardinghouse or hotel in town. When he walked into the Red Creek Saloon, he looked around the room to see every table with a bottle of whiskey on it. A few men lifted their glasses up at him. He walked to the bar and smiled at the barkeep.

"Any rooms left upstairs?"

"Yep, two dollars a night, three if you want a woman with it," he said. Jess handed him a five-dollar gold piece and the man took it.

"You want three women with the room?" he asked as he looked at the gold coin.

"No, just the room," Jess said.

The barkeep handed him the key and he headed up the stairs. As he unlocked the door to his room, a woman walked out from one of the other rooms. She combed her hair with her fingers and brushed her dress off as she smiled at him.

"How much did you pay for the room?" she asked him.

He spun his head around and smiled at her. "Two dollars," he said as he walked in and closed the door. She frowned and headed for the steps.

Jess put his things away and took a short nap. When he woke, he splashed some water on his face and wiped it off with a towel as he thought about Hades and the Roper brothers. He knew that they'd be looking for their missing men when they didn't return. They would probably send out at least two men to look for them and find out what happened and he didn't want to be responsible for what they might do to any of the townsfolk in Chilton.

He finished and opened his door, careful to look at the stairway before coming all the way out. The place was noisy and when he started down the steps, the noise dimmed quite a bit. As he reached the bottom of the steps, he saw the same woman who had spoken to him earlier sitting on a man's lap. The man was large and burly-looking and smoking a fat cigar. Jess knew he was watching him, but he ignored it and strolled to the bar. He ordered a whiskey and a meal. He was eating a piece of cheese and some bread when he heard the batwings squeaking. He turned his head to see who it was and as soon as he locked eyes with the man standing just inside the doors, they both recognized each other immediately.

"Jess Williams?" said the man before he turned and ran back through the doors.

"Reasoner McKendry?" said Jess as he heard boots thudding on the boardwalk outside.

He dropped the cheese, thumbed his hammer strap off and ran through the doors in time to see McKendry riding his horse out of town, turning to the south as soon as he rounded the last building.

"Damn it," Jess muttered to himself as he slipped his hammer strap back on and looked at the sun heading down over the western landscape. He walked back inside and back to the bar. Tom Bunch, the owner and barkeep, gave him a questioning look.

"Ain't you going after him?" he asked.

Jess nodded. "Yeah, but I'll wait until morning to start tracking him," he explained. "The sun is going down and I ain't giving him the opportunity to ambush me in the dark. I'll take that stew now." Jess felt the occasional stare of the big burly man while he ate his meal. He removed his hammer strap as a precaution.

CHAPTER TEN

Jess was saddling his horses in the morning when Marshal Schneider walked inside with an envelope of money in his hand. Jess turned to him and he handed him the envelope. Jess counted the money and found the entire four thousand dollars. He removed a one-hundred-dollar bill and handed it to the marshal.

"That's for your trouble," Jess told him.

"If you were paying me for my trouble, you'd hand over the entire four thousand," he remarked smartly.

"Sorry, Marshal, but you took the oath and pinned that badge on."

"I needed the money and everything was fine until the Roper brothers started showing up."

"Take the badge off and find another job."

"If I did that, my wife would leave me."

"I know a man by the name of Ollie who'd probably change places with you."

"You talking about Ollie Boran, the fighter?"

"Yeah, you know him?"

"Sure, he comes here once in a while to set up a fight. He's always complained about that women he's married to."

Jess shook his head at the memory. "Well, I gotta go, Marshal," he said as he climbed up into the saddle on Gray. "I have a man on the run and I'm heading out to get him."

"I heard. Are you bringing him back here?"

"Probably," he said as he nudged Gray into a walk along the street, his packhorse, Sharps, following faithfully behind.

When he reached the spot where McKendry turned his horse south the day before, he examined the tracks closely. He followed them for a quarter mile before determining they were McKendry's tracks. He nudged Gray into a moderate gallop, keeping a watchful eye on the trail ahead.

His thoughts turned to McKendry. He was well known as a back shooter and an ambusher, which is why Jess was taking it a little more slowly than normal. He rode way around several places that could be ambush spots, but nothing happened. He noticed that the tracks turned from south to southwest as if he were traveling in a wide circle. After a while, the tracks turned northward.

Jess stopped and looked around the area. "I wonder if he's heading to Hades," he whispered to himself.

* * *

Jacob Powell stood guard on top of the saloon in Hades. It was late in the afternoon and he was sitting down whittling on a piece of wood to pass the time. He kept looking at the piece of wood, wondering what it was supposed to be, but he couldn't figure it out. He looked up every minute or so and eventually noticed movement far off on the hard rocky ground. He picked up his rifle and stood up, peering off in the distance with a pair of field glasses. He stomped on the roof three times to get the attention of the men inside. A few minutes later, Elam Roper came walking up the back steps to see what the stir was about.

"You'd better not have gotten me up here for nothing," Elam warned him.

"A horse and rider ain't nothing," he said as he pointed at the lone rider making his way through the rocky terrain.

Elam took the field glasses from Powell and watched for a few minutes. He grabbed Powell's rifle and aimed at the ground to the side of the rider. He fired one shot that echoed through the rocky hills surrounding the town.

The rider stopped in his tracks and threw his hands up in the air. "It's Reasoner McKendry!" he hollered.

Elam looked though the field glasses again and finally recognized McKendry after he took his hat off.

"Dang it if it ain't McKendry out there," he muttered as he waved at him to approach. McKendry started his horse again until he reached the rear of the saloon.

Lester Roper walked out and smiled at him. "What the hell are you doing here, McKendry?" he asked.

"I was over in Chilton late yesterday and I ran into that bounty hunter, Jess Williams." Lester said.

Roper glared at Lester suspiciously. "And you decided to lead him here?" he demanded.

"No, I covered my tracks through water and over rocky land," he said. "He won't find me."

"Then you don't know Williams very well," berated Lester. "He can track a man who can walk on water."

"Are you telling me I can't come into town?"

"No, I'm telling you that if you led him here, you won't have to worry about him killing you," Lester told him with deadly intent.

McKendry turned in the saddle and looked at his trail behind him and then turned back around. "I'll take my chances with you."

"Come on then," said Lester as he waved him in. McKendry rode his horse toward the rear of the saloon and dismounted. Lester frowned at him and pointed to the end building.

"Take your horse to the livery and come back here," he told him. McKendry nodded and headed along the back of the buildings toward the livery. Lester glanced up at Elam, who stood at the edge of the roof.

"Elam, keep your eyes peeled out the way McKendry rode in," he told him. "If Williams is trailing him, he might show up and he's the last person we need to come here."

"Sure thing, brother," he said. "Do you think maybe Williams ran into Rogan and Carmichael in Chilton?"

"Well, they ain't back yet, so either they got too drunk to return or something worse," advised Lester. "If they don't show up tonight, we'll go in tomorrow and find out what happened."

"You'd better send more than two men if Williams is hanging around there."

"Don't tell me how to run things. Have McKendry relieve you of your post when he comes back," cautioned Lester. Elam said nothing; he simply stood back from the edge and peered through the field glasses.

* * *

Jess continued tracking McKendry, but the rougher the terrain got, the harder it was for him to follow. He got sidetracked several times before getting back on the right track. It started to get dark and he knew he was getting close to the south side of Hades. The terrain was rough, but it did provide him good cover when he stopped near the creek McKendry had ridden through. He let his horses drink their fill and found a spot between some huge boulders where he could make the smallest fire possible to make coffee.

In the morning, he followed the creek in both directions and eventually found the spot where McKendry had come out. The only clues were a few broken pebbles and some sand that was out of place on the rocky terrain, obviously deposited by a horse's hoof. He followed along the spot he calculated McKendry would ride, since it was the only spot that wasn't riddled with rocks and stones. When he knew he was close to Hades, he headed up a small rise in the barren landscape and when he had almost reached the top, he dismounted and walked the rest of the way. When he looked down, he saw the blood-red buildings of the town.

"It even looks like hell," he whispered as he extended his spyglass and scanned the town.

He spotted two guards posted on top of buildings. One was on top of the saloon. The other was on the building right across from it. He focused on the guard on top of the saloon and realized it was McKendry. He sat down with his head peering over the edge of the rise he was on. His hat was on the ground beside him with some hardtack in it.

He kept watching for a few hours and noticed two other men relieving McKendry and the other guard on the rooftops. When that happened, he saw two men walking out of the back of the saloon. One lit up a thin cigar and the other relieved himself on a shed.

"That makes six men for certain," he whispered to himself. "Tomorrow, one of them dies."

CHAPTER ELEVEN

Lester Roper was in a foul mood the next morning after discovering Rogan and Carmichael still hadn't returned from Chilton with whiskey and supplies. That, along with the knowledge that Jess Williams might be involved, put him into a brooding state of mind. He finished breakfast and wiped his mouth off on his sleeve before looking over at Jacob Powell.

"Powell, take two men and ride into Chilton," he told him. "Find out what happened to Rogan and Carmichael, and if they're dead, kill that weasel of a town marshal there."

"Sure thing, boss," said Powell as he stood to leave.

"And bring some more damn whiskey," added Lester.

"Rivard, Winslow, you two are with me," barked Powell. The two men stood up, checked their pistols and followed Powell out of the saloon, heading for the livery.

Jess was sitting in the same spot on the rise outside town drinking coffee when he saw three men walking out of the saloon. He watched them go to the livery and come back out a little later with three saddled horses. The three men checked their rifles and slid them back into their scabbards. They headed out of town in the direction of Chilton, most likely to find out what had happened to Rogan and Carmichael.

"That doesn't look good," he muttered to himself as he watched them through his spyglass.

He folded it up and looked at one man walking out of the back of the saloon and onto the roof. He extended the spyglass. It was McKendry. A minute later, another man appeared on the roof of the building across from the saloon. He couldn't identify him, but he made the assumption that every man with the Roper brothers was either wanted by the law or surely should be.

His attention was distracted by some hollering and cursing. He moved the spyglass down to the street where two men were dragging another man out of the general store. His feet were dragging in the dirt as they hauled him toward the saloon. They stopped in front of it, not far from where the charred cross remained. They held the man there and McKendry and the other man on the rooftop walked to the fronts of the buildings to watch.

Down at the saloon, Elam walked out and Lester stayed in the doorway, both with evil smiles on their faces. The man from the general store was pleading and praying. He slowly looked up at Elam, who had stepped off the board-walk and up to him. Elam glared wolfishly at him.

"How come there ain't a new cross buried in the ground yet?" he demanded of the man, who shook his head in fear.

"We were going to put it up today, honest," he pleaded.

Elam looked over at the general store to see a woman standing there with her hands held in prayer and crying. "Is that your woman over there?" he asked.

The man turned his head and saw his wife standing in front of the store. "Yes, that is my wife," he said.

HADES

"Do you love her?"

"Huh?"

"I said, do you love her," yelled Elam.

"Of…of course I do."

"How much?"

"I don't understand," cried the man.

"Do you love her enough to give your life for hers?"

"Why are you doing this to us?" the man wailed.

Elam drew his pistol and whipped it across the man's face, opening a deep gash on his cheek. "You don't get to ask questions," he told him. "Now, do you love her enough to give your life to save her?"

The man swiveled his head back over to his wife and then back up to Elam. "Yes, I would give my life for her," he said as the blood dripped from his cheek.

Elam looked over at the woman, who stood there trembling. "Your man says he's willing to give his life for you," he called out to her.

She moved her hands from her face.

"Please, no," she begged. "Do not kill him, I beg of you. I will do anything you ask, anything."

Elam grinned at the two men holding the man. "Did you hear that?" he asked them. "She says she'll do anything I want if I don't kill him."

"We heard it, boss," said one of the men holding her husband. "Maybe you should take her up on her offer. She's not a bad-lookin' woman."

Elam bent over and put his face closer to the woman's husband. "Looks like your woman's got more gonads than you," he scoffed. "I'm gonna go and see exactly what she's willing to do to save your hide."

"No," wailed the man. "You can kill me! Just leave her be!" Elam stood up, holstered his pistol and headed for the store where the woman stood, her hands clasped in prayer.

"Damn it," whispered Jess as he stood up, walked back to his horses and pulled out both of his Sharps buffalo rifles.

He chambered a round into each of them and made his way back to his spot. He got on his stomach and moved a few rocks around. He lifted the sights on one of the rifles and checked the distance. The street was about four hundred yards away from his position. He began to sight in on Elam's backside, but he pushed the woman inside the store and followed behind her before Jess could fire.

He gently set the rifle down and picked up his spyglass and continued to watch. A few tense minutes later, Elam came walking back out of the general store buckling his gun belt back on. He walked over to the man on his knees and stood in front of him.

"You were gonna die for that?" he asked the man, who struggled against the two men holding him. "She didn't put up as much of a fight as you are now. I gotta tell you, Mister, she ain't worth dying for, but then again, what do I know about such things?"

"You're a filthy pig!" cursed the man as he spat on Elam's boots.

Elam pulled his pistol out, shoved it into the man's mouth and pulled the trigger. The two men holding him let go and stepped away as the man's brains splattered out of the back of his head. His lifeless body fell backward and his legs flopped out from underneath him.

The woman, half dressed, ran out of the general store screaming. She held a rifle in her hands and when she lifted it, McKendry raised his rifle and fired. The slug slammed into her chest, knocking her against the store's front wall. She slid down and slumped into a sitting position. Lester, who was still standing in the doorway, watched the whole affair unfold. He looked at his brother.

"If you keep killing what's left of the townsfolk, who's gonna do the cooking and cleaning?" he said.

"Don't worry, brother. There are a few women left in town," said Elam as he replaced the spent shell in his pistol. "What do you want us to do with these two bodies?" Lester looked over at the woman on the boardwalk, her bare chest all bloodied now.

"Have a couple of the men take her out of town and burn the body like she was a witch," ordered Lester. "Cut the man's head off and stick it on a pole out at the trail coming in from Chilton. That should scare off most people."

Elam ordered the two men to do what Lester said and headed for the saloon. They dragged the dead man's body over to the general store and picked up the body of the woman, then carried her down the street toward the trail going to Chilton.

Jess lay there with fury filling his body, looking for a place to escape. He had wanted to stop the killing, but it had all happened so fast. He hadn't expected the woman to come running out with a rifle. He made some quick calculations in his mind. Three men had ridden out earlier, two men were dragging the woman's body out of town and two men stood on the rooftops. He didn't know how many men were left inside the saloon, but at this moment, he didn't care.

He had done some scouting before dark yesterday and found the best escape route to use. He knew that once he started firing, the men inside the saloon would hunker down for a few minutes before attempting to come after him. That would give him enough time to make his escape. He figured he had two shots, one at McKendry and one at the other man on the roof across the street.

He propped the barrel of the rifle on top of a rock and peered through the sights. He aimed dead center at the back of McKendry, who sat on the raised edge of the building, looking around the town. He gently squeezed back on the trigger.

"You might think you're safe in Hades, but wait until you see hell for real," he whispered to himself as the rifle bucked and boomed.

Flames, smoke, lead and death were delivered to the spinal column in the center of McKendry's back. His body lurched and fell forward, bouncing off the covered roof once before landing in the dirt in a loud dusty thud. Before McKendry's body hit the dirt, Jess already had his other buffalo rifle in his hands, aiming at the other guard, who had run across the rooftop to see McKendry plunging down to the street. The man's eyes slowly looked up in Jess's direction where he could see the smoke rising in the air. He racked a shell into his rifle and was about to aim it in Jess's direction, when he saw the bright orange flames. The three hundred seventy-five grain slug slammed into the man's chest, knocking him off his feet and three feet back onto the rooftop. Inside the saloon, everyone jerked his pistol out and ducked down.

"Who in the hell is that shooting out there?" demanded Lester.

"I don't know, but it sounded like one of them buffalo rifles," said Elam.

"McKendry is down for sure," said one of the men as he looked out the front window of the saloon. "I don't see the guard on the roof across the street either."

"Who the hell would have the gonads to attack us?" asked Elam.

"I don't know, but whoever he is, he's a dead man," hollered Lester as he edged a look around a window in the back of the saloon. He saw the black smoke wafting in the wind.

"Whoever it was, he was shooting from up on that ridge behind the saloon," said Lester. "Elam, get the horses ready to ride." Elam ran out of the saloon and headed for the livery. The two men who had been dragging the woman's body along the trail to Chilton came running back. Elam waved at them to follow him to the livery.

Jess was already on Gray and running him as fast as he safely could, Sharps following behind. They made it to the creek and Jess rode in it a good mile before coming out the other side. He knew they'd come looking for him, but he was banking on his horses to allow him to get away. Once he hit the flatland, he rested them a bit and then put them into another fast gallop.

It took a good ten minutes before Lester, Elam and the other men got to the top ledge of the hill where the shooting had come from. When they reached it, Elam dismounted and looked around until he found two spent shells lying by the edge. He picked them up and examined them.

"I was right. These are fifty-caliber shells," he said as he threw them out into the air, letting them fall down the hillside. "That bounty hunter is known to use long-range buffalo rifles. Maybe McKendry didn't hide his tracks as well as he thought."

"Too bad I can't kill McKendry for leading him here," carped Lester.

He climbed back up in the saddle and led the group along the barren landscape until they reached the creek. They had found a few broken pebbles indicating a horse and rider, but when they looked on the other side of the creek, they saw nothing.

"He probably rode in the creek," surmised Elam. "It's what I'd do."

"Let's get back to town," grumbled Lester. "If it was Jess Williams, he planned his escape route well and we can't leave the town with only a few men guarding it. The locals might get the same idea that woman did and start shootin' at us."

Elam sighed and turned his horse around. "He may have gotten away with this, but I'll make sure he's dead before this is over," he said as he headed back to town, anger welling up inside him.

CHAPTER TWELVE

Marshal Schneider was heading for the café to get himself some lunch when he saw the three riders approaching the west end of Main Street. His heart skipped a beat when he realized it was three of Elam's men. The lump in his throat grew larger when he saw that one of the men was Jacob Powell, a man who was well known for his ruthless deeds.

He didn't know the other two men, Saul Rivard and Raif Winslow, but they looked just as mean. He stopped in the middle of the street, not because he wanted to, but because his feet became frozen to the ground as if the devil himself was holding him by the ankles. The three men rode straight up to him and stopped. Powell gently pushed his hat back on his head and leaned forward in the saddle.

"Afternoon, Marshal," drawled Powell.

"Good...afternoon," he said as he forced a nervous smile. Schneider glanced at the other two men who were both glaring at him and holding the butts of their pistols.

"You wouldn't happen to know the whereabouts of two of our men we sent into town for some supplies and whiskey, now do you?" Schneider stalled for a few seconds, trying to think of an answer that might not get him killed.

"Uh, yeah, they did come in and buy some supplies and whiskey, but they rode out of town heading east," he said briskly. "I thought that was kind of odd, but as you know, I don't interfere with the Ropers or their men."

Powell stared at him for a long time before speaking again. "East, eh?"

Schneider nodded his head. "Yeah, east," he said.

"Then, you wouldn't mind if we took a look at the local cemetery to see if there are any fresh graves?"

"Well, we did bury two of the local townsfolk lately," lied Schneider.

"Is that so?" asked Powell.

"Uh, yeah."

"Well, let's get a shovel and dig one up just to make sure it ain't Rogan or Carmichael," said Powell as one of the other men untied a shovel from the back of his saddle and threw it on the ground in front of Schneider.

He looked at the shovel and beads of sweat started trickling down the sides of his face. "I'll go and get the undertaker and tell him…"

"We don't need the undertaker," Powell said cleverly. "You know how to use a shovel, don't you?"

"But…"

"Pick up the shovel," ordered Powell as he drew his pistol and pointed it at him.

Schneider picked it up and turned toward the end of town where the cemetery was. Powell and the other two men walked their horses slowly behind the marshal. Some of the townsfolk peeked out of windows and half-open doorways. No one attempted to interfere, knowing it would bring them certain death. When Schneider reached the cemetery, he opened the wooden gate and stood there.

Powell saw two fresh graves and frowned. "Start digging," he ordered.

Schneider started digging and after a while, the shovel hit the wooden box. He continued to dig and the sweat was dripping off his face now. When he had the pine box uncovered, he turned to look at Powell with an anxious gaze.

"I didn't have anything to do with this," he spluttered.

Powell cocked his head and pointed the pistol at him. "Open the lid," he said. Schneider pulled the lid off to reveal a very dead Lowe Rogan inside the pine box.

"Well, well," sighed Powell. "Now how do you think that happened?"

"It was that bounty hunter, Jess Williams," blurted Schneider. "He killed them both. I wasn't there to stop him, but I would have, honest." Powell became alert at the mention of the name. Rivard and Winslow didn't seem to recognize it. Powell turned in the saddle and looked nervously back toward town.

"He ain't here," said Schneider. "I ran him out of town after I found out he did this."

Powell leered at Schneider. "No one could run Jess Williams out of town, especially a yellow, lily-livered coward like you. Get out of there and start walking toward that big oak tree."

Schneider looked at the tree close to the cemetery and he started to visibly tremble. "Why?" he stammered.

"I think you know why," said Powell in a foreboding manner.

"But I told you, I ran Williams out of town for doing this," he said imploringly.

"I know what you said," scoffed Powell. "I just don't believe one word of it. Now start walking."

Schneider stood there, his feet frozen to the ground again. He thought about going for his pistol, but he knew it was futile against the three gunmen.

Powell fired one slug that missed his head by a few inches. "I said, start walking," he told him. "If not, there will be two bodies in that hole, only one won't be in a pine box and he won't be dead when we throw the dirt on him."

Schneider knew he was all out of options, unless he wanted to go for his gun and get filled with lead. The only reason he decided against it was the threat that Powell made about burying him alive. They'd shoot him in both arms and legs and shovel the dirt on top of him. The thought of dying that way scared the wits out of him.

He stepped out of the hole and slowly walked toward the tree, his head and shoulders slumped. Powell kept his gun trained on him and Rivard began fixing a hangman's noose with a coil of rope. Winslow slid from the saddle and threw the noose end of the rope over a heavy branch. Then, he walked over and tied the other end of it to the saddle horn on Powell's horse. Schneider stood there praying to himself as a few townsfolk began to gather around.

Powell looked at them and waved them over. "Come closer," he said. "See what happens when anyone in this town crosses any of us."

Winslow removed Schneider's hat and put the crude noose around his neck and tightened it slowly. Powell smiled maliciously at Schneider as he started backing his horse up. Schneider felt the noose tighten and he was lifted up onto his toes. Powell let him stay that way for a few moments before backing his horse up some more.

Schneider's feet lifted off the ground and he started to struggle and claw at the rope. His face turned beet red as the noose tightened even more. As he started to feel the wooziness from lack of air, he made one last attempt to draw his pistol, but Powell shot him in his right arm, causing him to drop it. It didn't take long before the struggling stopped and Schneider's body became limp. He hung there with his eyes bulging out. Powell heard hushed whispering going on in the small crowd behind him. He looked at Winslow as he moved his horse forward to loosen the tension on the rope.

"Pull him back off his feet, tie this end of the rope to another branch and leave him hanging there," he told Winslow as he untied the rope from his saddle horn and threw it to him. Schneider's body slumped to the ground.

Winslow found a branch stiff enough. He pulled on the rope until Schneider's body was just off the ground again and then he tied it around the branch. Winslow climbed up in the saddle and the three gunmen turned around to the small crowd that had gathered.

"You better tell everyone else in this town that this is what happens when you cross us," Powell told them as if he were preaching a sermon.

The owner of the Red Creek, Tom Bunch, stepped forward. "But we didn't have anything to do with your men being killed," he said sheepishly.

Powell leaned forward in his saddle, his pistol still in his hand. "The marshal said it was the bounty hunter Jess Williams who killed them," said Powell.

"Yeah, that's right."

"Are you certain it was Williams?"

"Yeah, Jess Williams."

Powell sat straight up in the saddle. "How can you be so sure?"

"Well, he signed his name on the paperwork for the marshal," said Bunch. "I saw the signature with my own eyes. The marshal was real upset about the whole matter."

Powell glanced over his shoulder at the body swaying in the breeze. "He ain't upset about it anymore," he said. "Now get on back to what you were doing and don't cut this body down. If I come back here and that body ain't hanging there, I'll kill two of you and it won't matter which two."

The crowd quickly dispersed and Rivard rode up next to Powell. "So, who is this Jess Williams?" he asked.

"He's the worst thing that could happen to us," Powell explained. "Let's just pray that he's moved on."

"Maybe he trailed McKendry to Hades," said Rivard.

"Then we'd best get back pronto," ordered Powell. "Let's fill our saddlebags with whiskey and get back to town."

They stopped at the saloon, packed their saddlebags with whiskey bottles and stopped at the general store to get some food supplies. They tied large bags to their saddle horns. As they were finishing, the livery worker brought them the wagon that Rogan and Carmichael had brought to town with them. They quickly untied the bags and placed them in the back of the wagon. Winslow climbed up in the front seat after securing his horse to the back. They rode out of town and most of the townsfolk watched them leave.

Bunch was standing in front of the saloon with two other men. "Let's pray they never return," he said as he glanced over at Schneider's limp body swaying in the breeze.

One of the other men looked over at it and grunted. "I say we pray that the bounty hunter who killed their men finds the rest of them," he said hopefully.

CHAPTER THIRTEEN

Jess was scanning the area behind him with his spyglass to make sure no one was following. He rested his horses for a few minutes and then put Gray into an ever-increasing gallop until he was at a full-out run with Sharps right behind him. He rode in a semi-circle, heading southeast until he hit a shallow river. He rode in the water for two miles before coming out and heading northeast toward Chilton, trying to hide his tracks from any of Elam's men who might follow him.

Before he rode into town, he saw a body hanging from an oak tree swaying in the breeze. The vultures were constantly flapping their wings in an attempt to dispose of the rotting corpse. Jess rode closer and saw the badge pinned to the torn and tattered shirt. The large ugly birds soared into the air waiting to return to their meal. Jess shook his head and let out a long frustrated sigh, feeling somewhat responsible for the marshal's death. If he had stayed in town, maybe he could have prevented it.

He rode his horses to the livery and handed the reins over to the worker, who didn't even look up at him. He took his things and headed for the Red Creek Saloon. When he pushed through the batwing doors, all the men inside lowered their heads and became silent. Tom Bunch stood behind the bar with his arms folded across his chest. Jess walked up to him and placed his things on the table closest to him.

"I suppose you want a room again?" asked Bunch.

"Yeah."

"How long you staying this time?" he asked somewhat sarcastically.

"I already feel bad enough about the marshal getting his neck stretched," Jess told him.

Bunch shook his head and gave him an apologetic look. "Hell, I suppose it ain't really your fault," he admitted. "Those men could have come in and killed any of us for any reason they could think up."

"If it's any consolation, I killed two more of them this morning," Jess said, as he lowered his head and shook it while remembering the killing of the husband and wife from the general store.

"It's not worth much, unless you plan on killing every last one of them," said Bunch.

Jess looked up at him with a look in his eyes that would scare the life out of most men. "I plan to do exactly that," he told Bunch plainly. "And after I kill every one of Elam's men, I'm going to kill him and his brother. When I'm finished, Hades will get a new name and the town will be painted all white. I won't quit until it's done."

"I reckon if anyone can do it, it'd be you," acknowledged Bunch.

"Does anyone in town sell dynamite?"

"Why? What do you need with dynamite?"

"They changed the name of that town to Hades, so I'm gonna make them think it actually is."

"I think the general store has a few cases of the stuff in their shed behind the store," advised Bunch.

"Thanks," Jess said sullenly as he climbed the steps to the rooms upstairs.

He put his things in his room and meticulously cleaned all his weapons. When he finished, he went downstairs and had a meal and a few drinks. He slowly put together a plan in his head. He had the barkeep pencil out a map of Hades and the four trails leading in and out of it. The town was surrounded by craggy uneven terrain and each trail fell off with steep ledges on both sides. The only trail wide enough for anything but a single rider was the one that led from Chilton to Hades. He folded the map, put it into his pocket and walked up to his room and retired for the night, thinking about the killing of the two townsfolk in Hades and Marshal Schneider's body swaying in the breeze out by the cemetery.

* * *

Rivard, Powell and Winslow trotted back into Hades in the late afternoon. As they rode in from the direction of Chilton, they saw the burned remains of the woman from the general store hanging from a wooden cross on the side of the trail just outside town. A sign was nailed to a stick that was pounded into the ground. The sign read: "Another witch is dead." They stopped and looked at the remains.

"That oughta scare the wits out of people who come this way," chuckled Powell.

"Do you think there really are witches and demons?" asked Winslow who sat in the seat of the wagon. Powell and Rivard swiveled their heads around to him and frowned.

"Hell, no," declared Powell. "But some people still believe in 'em."

"Not me," said Rivard.

They started up again and headed for town. Winslow kept staring at the burned corpse and he could have sworn that the woman's right index finger moved slightly. A shiver ran up his spine and he quickly looked straight away. As they rode to the saloon, Lester stood in the doorway. He looked directly at Powell.

"Boss wants to speak with you right now," he said briskly.

Powell nodded and slid from the saddle. He wrapped the reins to his horse around the hitch rail and walked inside the saloon. Elam was sitting at a table by himself and smoking a fat cigar. He inhaled the smoke and blew it up at the ceiling, watching the smoke wafting in the air. His eyes fell on Powell's as his head slowly lowered.

"I take it since Rogan and Carmichael didn't ride in with you that they're dead?" he asked.

Powell nodded his head. "Dead as the dirt keeping them warm," he replied.

"Was it that bounty hunter who did it?" asked Elam.

"That was the marshal's explanation, just before we stretched his neck."

"That sumbitch has killed four of our men so far and we haven't even seen him yet," said Lester.

Powell gave Elam a grave look. "Boss, I know the men we have in town are all hardened gunmen, but this Jess Williams fellow is a real hard case and persistent as they come," he said with a look of caution. "The way I heard it, once he fixes his sights on something or someone, he never stops until he gets the job done. He's cagey and smart too."

Elam gave Powell an uncaring expression as he took another long drag on the cigar and blew the smoke up to the ceiling. "He's still only one man," Elam said calmly. "We've got nearly a dozen hard cases in town with us. Make sure you keep guards posted at all times."

"I will, but he killed the last two guards," said Powell.

Elam quickly became annoyed, his temper rising. "Then tell them to be more careful," he barked loudly.

Powell sighed and stood up. "Okay, boss," he said. "I'll take care of it personally."

"Good. You do that," Elam said contentiously.

Powell walked outside and called over to some of the men. He started giving orders to them about guard duty. Lester sat down across from his brother and waved at the barkeep to bring him a bottle of whiskey just as Rivard and Winslow walked in carrying heavy bags of food supplies and more whiskey. Lester poured some in two glasses and took a sip.

"What do you think about this Jess Williams feller?" Lester asked Elam.

"Like I said, he's only one man," replied Elam. "He's just another bounty hunter out to make a living killing our kind. If he comes back here, we'll show him what tough is."

"That's right, brother," cackled Lester. "He can't mess with the Roper brothers." Lester lifted his glass and tipped his head back, downing the amber liquid in one gulp.

CHAPTER FOURTEEN

The morning found Jess at the general store buying all the things he needed. He carefully packed the dynamite and the long coil of fuses in the saddlebags on Sharps. He had the clerk order dozens of cans of white paint. The clerk looked confused about it all, but he kept his mouth shut and did what was asked of him. Jess paid him and walked out. He looked up and down the street and saw several men and women watching him. He wondered what they were thinking and whether they knew what he was planning. Tom Bunch stood in front of the saloon with his arms folded and an expectant look on his face. Jess nodded at him and Bunch nodded back as if they both understood one another.

Jess climbed up in the saddle and headed out the west end of town on the wide trail that led toward Hades. He slowly made his way, looking down at the wagon ruts that were still plainly visible. When he began hitting the rocky uneven terrain, he slowed his horses to a walk, not wanting either of them to get injured. He saw the burned remains of the woman still tied to the charred wooden cross and stopped and took his spyglass out. He scanned the entire area thoroughly and saw nothing. He noticed the tall ridges on both sides of the trail. He slid from the saddle and took one of the sticks tied to the back of Sharps' saddle with the sign he had painted in red letters that had the name Hades crossed out. The name *"Hell"* was written in red paint below that. He used a rock to pound it into some soft dirt.

He turned his horses off the trail and rode to the south side of Hades. He stopped often when he got close enough to scan the town with his spyglass and make notes on the map that Bunch had drawn for him. He used a stubby pencil to mark areas on the map, working on his plan as he did. He stopped near the trail where the head of the man from the general store in Hades sat atop a stick pounded in the dirt. He looked around and found the narrowest part of the trail close to the man's head. On both sides sheer rock ledges stood consisting of brownish red rock that was made up of what looked like a porous material. All the rocky ledges that surrounded Hades like pillars of death were made of the same material. It was as if they once rose up from hell out of the flat land that surrounded the town.

He spent the next few days cautiously riding around the outskirts of town, making mental notes as well as written ones on the map. He noted escape routes that would quickly take him out to the flat land when he needed. As he did, he left small bundles of dynamite hidden under rocks, knowing he would need them later. He pounded in a sign at each of the other three trails leading in and out of Hades. He slept under one ledge that provided him some cover where he could make a small fire for coffee. He ate cold meals consisting of beans, peaches and jerky.

The light mist of the third morning was still evident in the air as he sat between two ledges scanning the town with his spyglass. The place was eerily quiet. No one stirred this early in the morning, not even the local townsfolk who remained. Most of them were too afraid to come out in the open for fear they'd lose their lives to one of Elam's men.

He saw the saloon and watched as one man walked out and relieved himself. He didn't know who it was, but he didn't care. He didn't even care about collecting the bounty on the killers' heads at this point. The money wasn't important. Releasing the evil grip the gunslingers and killers had on the town was all that mattered to him now.

He stood up and walked back to his horses. He rode them to the sign he had placed on the trail. He made sure the signs only faced toward the town. Nothing was written on the opposite sides.

He slid from the saddle and began to carefully tie a rope across the trail near the sign. He tied it to two rocky ledges. Then, he meticulously tied a bundle of wooden matchsticks and the end of the fuse underneath the rope with a piece of string.

He secured it so that when the rope was jerked, the matchsticks would slide against the rock and ignite the short fuse that was attached to the three sticks of dynamite tied to the same ledge. When he was sure he had the matchsticks adjusted correctly, he looked at his work to make sure it was satisfactory. The rope running across the trail was at a height that would miss a horse's head, but catch a rider's head or neck. He climbed back up in the saddle and rode to the spot he had picked out that allowed him a quick escape. It had a good view of the town and the back of the saloon. He climbed from the saddle and pulled out the Sharps rifle from the scabbard on Gray and chambered a shell into it. He knelt down and propped the rifle on a rock and watched the back of the saloon again.

"Let's hope someone else has to relieve himself soon," he whispered to himself. He bit off a piece of jerky and chewed on it, watching and waiting patiently. He saw a man walking out of the back door, but he was wearing an apron and no weapon.

"Must be the barkeep," he whispered to himself.

He waited another half hour and then a man wearing a gun on his right hip walked out of the back door. Jess quickly picked up his spyglass and peered through it. He recognized him as one of the men who had dragged the man from the general store into the street in front of the saloon. He put the spyglass down and aimed through the sights of the rifle. He calculated the distance and aimed his sights just above the man's head. He slowly squeezed back on the trigger until the rifle exploded, the boom echoing several times off the rocky ledges and craggy pillars surrounding the town.

The custom-loaded three hundred seventy-five grain slug picked the man off his feet and he hit the dirt flat on his back in a dusty thud. Most of the men inside the saloon were still sleeping off their drunken stupor from the night before. Elam Roper flew out of his room with his pistol in his hand and wearing only his long johns.

"What the hell just happened!" he hollered. A few more doors flew open and some of the men downstairs drinking coffee ducked behind overturned tables. Lester was behind the bar with his pistol in his hand. He looked up at Elam excitedly.

"Someone just kilt Stumpy," hollered one of the men by the back door of the saloon.

"Stumpy is dead?" Elam responded.

"He's out behind the saloon in a pool of blood and he ain't gettin' up," he hollered up to Elam.

"That sounded like one of those buffalo rifles again," added Lester from behind the bar.

"Lester, take three men and ride up there and kill that bastard," ordered Elam. "It's probably that damn bounty hunter again."

Lester picked out three of the men and they headed for the livery. It didn't take long before the four of them rode out of town, all carrying rifles and cross expressions on their faces. Jess watched them from his spot and when he saw them coming toward him, he calmly stood up, walked to his horses and slid the rifle back into its scabbard. He climbed up in the saddle and rode along the trail. When he reached the rope that he had stretched so tightly, he ducked down and rode underneath it.

He went another three hundred yards past the rope and dismounted. He slid the Sharps rifle out again and chambered another round into it. He moved his horses out of the line of fire and leaned up against one of the rocky ledges and waited.

Lester led the other three men up to the area where they'd heard the shot come from. There was no smoke left in the air to pinpoint exactly where the shot had been taken. Lester looked at one of the other men.

"Ride farther along that trail and see if you find anything," he ordered.

The man heeled his horse along the trail and when he got closer to the stretched rope, Jess momentarily stepped out from behind the ledge and showed himself. The man saw him and spurred his horse faster as he racked a shell into his rifle. Jess stepped back behind the ledge and waited. The man was concentrating on the spot where he had seen Jess momentarily show himself. He turned his head in the saddle and called out to Lester.

"The sumbitch is over here," he hollered just before the rope caught the side of his face, pulling him out of the saddle and onto the rocky ground.

The rope jerked when it happened and the bundle of matches scraped across the rough rock and ignited the short fuse. The horse continued on along the trail and went past Jess. The man slowly stood up and felt his chin as Lester and the other two men started heading his way. He looked at Lester and thumbed behind him.

"He's behind a ledge about three hundred yards that way," he said excitedly just before the bundle of dynamite exploded.

Lester was looking at the man one second. The next second, all he saw was a fireball. He felt himself being blown off his horse by the blast of air that followed. Rocks and pieces of dirt fell on him and the other two men who were also on the ground.

"What the hell!" wailed Lester. He tried to stand up as a piece of arm slammed into the ground in front of him.

He stood up and helped the man closest to him stand as they tried to look past the pile of rubble that closed off the trail now. Jess edged around the ledge he was behind and waited for the dust to settle enough to see anything. When it did, he aimed at one of the men who was brushing himself off. He squeezed the trigger until the buffalo rifle bucked and bellowed. The heavy-caliber slug punched a hole in the man's chest, knocking him back on the ground, dead when he hit it.

Jess immediately climbed up in the saddle and followed the path he had picked out beforehand. Lester and the other man jumped behind a boulder and waited for a long minute, wondering if another explosion was about to occur. Once they felt it was safe, they slowly walked out and looked at the pile of rubble that closed off the trail.

They walked around the rubble and found a few more pieces of the man who had been knocked off his horse by the rope. When Lester saw the sign Jess had pounded into the ground and read it, his eyes narrowed and his features hardened. He raised his rifle and fired several slugs into the sign, all the while yelling at the top of his lungs.

"You crazy son of a bitch!" he screamed. "When we catch you, we're gonna take a week to kill you!" He stopped firing at the sign and looked at the other man, who had a worried look on his face as he stared at the bullet-riddled sign that said "Hell" on it.

"It can't be just one man doing all this," the man said, his voice sounding grave and apprehensive.

"Did you get a look at him at all?" asked Lester.

The man shook his head quickly. "You mean between gettin' blown off my horse, seeing body parts falling and watching our man catch a bullet, all the while getting pounded with rocks and dirt?"

"Yeah," replied Lester.

"No," he said bluntly. Lester flipped his rifle around, holding it by the barrel and started slamming it into the rocky ground until one side of the butt stock fell off. He threw the rifle up in the air.

"Damn you to hell!" was the last thing Jess heard as he hit the flatland and urged Gray into a fast gallop along the same semi-circular path he had taken before.

CHAPTER FIFTEEN

Lester and his companion returned to town where the other men waited. Some were standing outside and some were inside the saloon with Elam. When Lester walked in, Elam stood up, still in his long johns.

"Well?" demanded Elam.

"I lost two men and never saw hide nor hair of him," admitted Lester.

"What the hell was that explosion?"

"He had some dynamite set up. Shit blew one of our men to pieces and knocked the rest of us clean off our horses."

"And you never saw him?"

"I told you I didn't," hollered Lester. "Then, before the dust settled, he plugged another man before he disappeared into thin air."

"He just disappeared?"

"Don't get me any madder than I already am," Lester warned his brother. "I told you, we never saw him, except for our man who got blown to pieces and unless we find his head, he ain't talking. I have to assume it was that damn bounty hunter Williams." Winslow, who stood by the bar listening, raised his hand. Elam saw it and jerked his head around to him.

"What, Winslow?" barked Elam.

"I was just thinkin' that maybe with all the stuff we've been doing to this town, maybe some demon really did come here," he said nervously. Elam picked up the bottle of whiskey from the table and threw it at Winslow. He ducked in time for the bottle to fly past him and slam into the wall.

"You danged imbecile," shouted Elam. "There ain't no such things as demons!"

"Sorry, boss, I was just thinkin'," he said apologetically.

"Let me do the thinkin' for this bunch," Elam yelled as he slumped back down in his chair. He sat there holding his pistol in his hand. Lester sat down across from his brother.

"The trail heading west out of town is of no use any-more," he informed Elam. "It's buried underneath a pile of rubble. The only way to ride west out of here is to ride slowly around the ledges and rocky pillars and that's slow going with all the rocky ground. And, the sumbitch put up a new sign on the trail too."

"What sign?"

"One that says Hades, which is crossed out with the word 'Hell' written below it," he explained. "It faces toward the town as if to say if we try to leave, we'll be heading to 'Hell.'"

"Why would he do that?"

"I think he's tryin' to send us a message," explained Lester.

Elam shrugged it off by waving his hands in the air. "He ain't sendin' us anything and we still have three more clean trails we can use." He reached over and grabbed a bottle of whiskey from one of the other men and took a long pull from it. He slammed the bottle down on the table and looked at the barkeep, Blake Archer, who stood by the doorway going to the back kitchen.

"Get in the back and start cooking breakfast," Elam ordered. "All this thinkin' is makin' me hungry." Everyone started walking outside and Winslow found a seat in a corner. He kept glancing down at the floor, fully expecting a demon to reach up and grab him by his boots.

* * *

Tom Bunch was wiping down the bar when the single rider rode by the Red Creek Saloon in Chilton. He rode tall in the saddle and was nicely dressed. What caught his attention though, was the shiny Colt fastened to the man's right leg. It was adorned with pearl handles and held in place by a black holster. The top of it was cut away to allow easier access to the hammer and the bottom of it was open, allowing the end of the barrel to protrude from it. Bunch watched him ride to the livery and come out a few minutes later carrying a rifle and small saddlebags.

The man headed straight for the saloon and stopped when he saw the body hanging from the oak tree, swaying in the breeze. Most of the flesh had been stripped off Schneider's body and the face was totally unrecognizable now. He stood there for a long moment staring at it before lowering his head and heading for the saloon again.

His spurs jingled as he walked up the steps and onto the boardwalk. He hesitated at the batwings as he gazed around the town once more. He looked disheveled as if he'd been riding the long trail. His keen eyes scanned all the men inside before pushing through the swinging doors. They clapped together behind him several times before becoming silent and still. He slowly made his way to the bar and placed his saddlebags on the floor, leaning his rifle on the bags. Bunch noticed that the hammer strap was removed from the pistol now. He also noticed the scar that ran from his right cheek to the corner of his mouth.

"Whiskey," he said in a deep raspy voice.

Bunch poured some in a glass and pushed it close to him. The man lifted the glass and tipped his head back, downing the amber liquid in one swallow. He slowly placed the glass back down on the bar and tapped it with his finger, letting Bunch know to refill it. He did and the man reached into his pocket and placed three dollars on the bar.

"Rooms?" he asked.

"Two dollars a night, three if you want a woman," Bunch told him.

"Don't have the time nor the inclination for a woman at the moment," he said sullenly. Bunch placed the key to one of the rooms upstairs on the bar. The man reached for it and put his left hand on Bunch's, holding it down against the bar.

"Who is that hanging from the tree by the cemetery?" he asked forcefully.

"What's left of it used to be our town marshal."

"Any new graves in the cemetery?"

"A few."

"Any of them have the name Arron Carmichael on it?"

"I believe one of them is a man named Carmichael, but they didn't put any grave markers on them." The man released Bunch's hand, picked up his glass and took a sip of the whiskey.

"Get the undertaker to dig them up so I can check for myself," the man said in a firm tone, indicating it wasn't a request. Bunch nodded at one of the men inside and he ran out through the batwings. A few minutes later, a man walked in holding a shovel. The man at the bar turned around to see him standing there.

"I was told you want some graves dug up," said the undertaker.

"I need you to uncover all the fresh graves in the cemetery," he said.

"It costs a dollar for each one."

"Start digging," he said. "I'll be out there shortly."

The undertaker glanced at Bunch to see if the man was good for the money and Bunch nodded. He turned and walked out, heading for the cemetery. The man finished his whiskey and picked up his saddlebags and rifle. He started up the steps to the rooms. Bunch looked up at him.

"Whose name should I put down on my ledger?" he asked the man. The man stopped and looked down at Bunch.

"Jason. Jason Carmichael," he said as he continued up the steps and went inside his room.

"Shit," muttered Bunch as he shook his head.

After a short while, Bunch heard the door creak open upstairs. Jason Carmichael walked down the steps and out through the batwings without saying a word. Bunch could hear the jingling of Carmichael's spurs scraping along the boardwalk as he walked toward the cemetery at the end of town. When he reached the cemetery, he saw one grave open and two men digging up a second one. Both men had rags tied over their noses due to the stench coming from what was left of Schneider's body swaying in the breeze. Carmichael removed a handkerchief from his back pocket and held it over his nose as he walked up to the first uncovered pine box. The lid had been removed and when he looked down into it, he removed the handkerchief from his nose. At first, his face seemed to loosen, but after a few seconds, his features sharpened.

"I'm sorry, brother," he said to the dead body of his brother Arron. "I will avenge your death and kill the man who put you in the ground." The undertaker and the other man stopped digging. Carmichael looked at them and forced a smile, the scar curling his lip up strangely as he did.

"Cover them back up," he said. "I saw all I need to see." He walked over and handed the undertaker five dollars.

"Make a grave marker for this one and put the name Arron Carmichael on it," he told him.

The undertaker nodded and Carmichael walked back toward the saloon. When he walked in, Bunch stood behind the bar. Carmichael nodded at his empty glass and Bunch poured some more whiskey in it.

"So, who is the man who killed my brother?" he asked Bunch directly.

CHAPTER SIXTEEN

Jess rode to the same river that he had ridden in before. He went in the opposite direction for a few miles and then out the other side. He headed straight south for a while and then turned back toward Chilton, hoping to throw off any of Elam's men who might try tracking him. When he rode back into Chilton, he headed for the livery. The owner walked out holding a shovel.

"How long you stayin'?" he asked.

"Just for the day," he told him. "I need you to put new shoes on both my horses." The man picked up one of Gray's front legs and examined the shoe.

"These look pretty new," he said.

"They are, but change them anyway."

"Why?"

"Just do it," Jess told him firmly as he pitched him a ten-dollar gold piece. The man caught it and put it into his pocket. "And watch my stuff for me."

"Okay, I'll get right on it, since all I have to do is muck stalls," he said. Jess started to turn when the man cleared his throat.

"Uh, you should know that someone is in town looking for you."

Jess stopped and slowly turned back to him. "Who?"

"Tom Bunch says he's the brother of one of the men you sent to the cemetery."

"Got a name?"

"Jason Carmichael."

"That didn't take long," said Jess as he slipped his hammer strap off and headed out of the livery.

Jess knew that Carmichael's brother would be looking for him eventually, but he didn't think it would happen so quickly. He wanted to pick up some more supplies and get back to Hades, but he would have to deal with Jason Carmichael first. He knew that an enraged brother bent on revenge wouldn't wait. He headed straight for Red Creek, assuming that was where Carmichael would be. He approached cautiously, checking rooftops and buildings, not knowing if he would be an ambusher or not.

When he reached the saloon, two local men walked out. They gave him a look that told him there was trouble waiting for him inside. He waited until the two locals walked away before pushing through the batwing doors. He quickly scanned the inside, but didn't see anything or anyone who was a threat. He looked at Bunch standing behind the bar and he was pointing to the rooms upstairs. Jess nodded and walked up to the bar.

"I hear that Carmichael's brother Jason is here looking for me?" Jess asked.

"Yeah, he's upstairs taking a nap," advised Bunch.

"How long has he been here?"

"Rode in today and had the undertaker uncover his brother's grave so he could be sure."

"And he knows I killed him?"

"Weren't no reason to lie about it," he replied. "We have enough problems with the Ropers and their men."

"There's two more of them in hell now."

"You killed two more of them?"

"Yeah."

"And you came back here?" Bunch asked with a hint of anger in his voice.

"Just to get more dynamite, but now I have him to take care of," he said as he darted his eyes up to the rooms on the second floor.

"You need more dynamite?"

"Yeah," he said as they both heard a door creak open upstairs.

Jess backed up toward the wall at the end of the bar and waited. There were a few heavy footsteps and then the first step coming down creaked slightly. Jess and Bunch watched as the two boots appeared, followed by the legs and then the torso of the man walking down the steps. Carmichael was halfway down when he looked over at the bar and saw Jess standing there.

He didn't know Jess by sight, but he knew of his reputation and made a quick calculation that it was either him or some other gunslinger just by the looks of him and all the guns he wore, especially the unique one that sat on his right leg. He slipped his hammer strap off and continued down the steps until he reached the bottom. He surveyed the room quickly and then turned his attention to Jess.

"You the man who killed my brother Arron Carmichael?" he asked bluntly.

"I am," replied Jess, making no attempt to avoid it.

"I'm his brother Jason. I suppose you know why I'm here."

"I do."

Carmichael slowly strolled to the bar, keeping his right hand away from his pistol, which Jess thought odd. Bunch poured him a whiskey and Carmichael picked up the glass and took a sip of it. He set the glass down and pursed his lips up.

"That shit's horrible," he said.

"Why don't you drink the good stuff?" Jess asked. Carmichael looked at him and smiled slightly, the scar curling his lips up again.

"I suppose I can clean out your pockets after I kill you so I can afford it, since my brother was worth three thousand dollars the last I heard."

"And the man he was with was worth one thousand," Jess told him.

"You got the money on you?"

"Yep."

"Then, not only am I going to kill the man who killed my brother, I'm going to get rich doing it."

"You're forgetting one small thing."

"Oh, and what is that?"

"You can't beat me."

"Is that so?"

"Yep."

"Did my brother draw on you first?"

"Yeah, right along with the man with him."

"And you took them both at the same time?"

"That's how it happened."

"I don't believe you," he scoffed, unconvinced.

"Ask the barkeep. He saw it since it happened right outside the batwings of his establishment."

Carmichael turned his head to Bunch with a questioning look on his face. "Is he telling the truth?" he asked Bunch, who nodded his head.

"I saw it all from where I'm standing right now," he told Carmichael. "I saw your brother and the other man outside the doors and I saw Jess through that window to the right of the doors. Your brother and the other man both went for their pistols first, but they never got them out of their holsters. I heard two shots, but they were so close together, you could hardly tell." Carmichael lowered his head in thought as if contemplating what his next move would be. Then, his face tightened and he raised his head up at Jess.

"I'll take that good whiskey now," he said without looking at Bunch. He reached behind him and poured a glass of good whiskey. Carmichael picked it up, took a sip of it and smiled.

"Damn, I'm gonna like drinking the good stuff from now on," he said.

"You do realize that from now on ends today, don't you?" asked Jess.

"You're that certain you can beat me?"

"Yep."

"You know it don't matter now, since you killed my brother and I'm obligated to avenge his death."

"You don't have to do it," said Jess.

"I wouldn't be a man if I didn't."

"Listen, your brother was a cold-blooded killer who was involved with two of the worst men breathing air, Lester and Elam Roper," explained Jess. "They've burned two women on wooden crosses claiming they were witches and they've murdered countless others for the sole purpose of keeping anyone from coming to their hideout in Hades."

"Hades, you say?" asked Carmichael, a surprised look washing across his face.

"Yeah, I don't know what they used to call the town, but everyone calls it Hades now," Jess told him.

"I thought that story was just that, a story," he said skeptically.

"I did too until I found out the truth and saw what was going on there with my own eyes."

"Is it really cursed like they say?"

"Not really. They've done a lot of things to make people believe the town is cursed and full of demons and witches. But the truth is, it's full of killers and thugs who don't want the law coming there. You can't even find the town on a map anymore."

"And my brother was working with the Ropers?"

"Yes, and who knows what he did to the innocent townsfolk in that town?"

"So why are you telling me all this?" Carmichael asked.

"Because I don't think you really want to do this."

"You don't think I want to avenge my brother's death?"

"Oh, I think you want to do exactly that. But why not avenge your brother's death against the men who are really responsible for him being a cold-blooded killer?" he proposed. "The Roper brothers and their killers would have gotten him killed sooner or later for certain. The only reason it happened sooner is because I found him in Hades and followed him to this town."

"But you're still the one who killed him," argued Carmichael.

"I'll admit, I pulled the trigger, but the people who are really responsible for his death are the Roper brothers."

Carmichael slowly shook his head as he thought about it. He still felt obligated to avenge his brother's death, but he knew that Arron had turned to the owl hoot trail years ago even though he had tried his best to talk him out of it. He picked up the glass of whiskey and downed it. He set the glass back down and looked back over at Jess.

"So, if I'm hearing you correctly, instead of me going up against you, you're suggesting I help you kill the Ropers and their gang?" he asked with a conflicted look on his face.

Jess looked at him shrewdly. "I can see the way your holster is worn from that Colt being pulled out more than a few times, along with the way the top is cut away for an easier draw. I know when I see a seasoned gunslinger, and I also know when I see one who has enough sense to think before he jerks for his iron. You've got skills and I can use your help. If you want to face me down later, I'll gladly oblige you. I give you my word on the matter. If you agree to work with me, I'll split the bounty money on the ones whose corpses we can actually turn in."

Carmichael thought about it while he poured himself another shot of the good whiskey. "You say that other man who was with my brother when you killed him was worth one thousand dollars?"

"He was."

"And you got paid?"

"Yeah, which is the reason the town marshal got hanged out by the cemetery."

"I saw that."

"Just one more reason the Ropers have to be taken down."

"Then give me half of the bounty up front."

"You want two thousand dollars without lifting a finger?"

"No, I want five hundred from the other man. I don't want any of the money you collected on my brother. If you want my help, that's the deal. Take it or leave it."

Jess counted out five hundred dollars and placed it on the bar with his left hand. Carmichael's left hand covered the money and Jess's hand, both of them with their right hands near the butt of their pistols. They stared into each other's eyes for a long moment, the tension growing slightly. Carmichael let go of Jess's hand and grabbed the money.

"One more thing," concluded Carmichael.

"What?"

"I still reserve the right to brace you when this is over with," he said with meaning.

"We have a deal then?"

"We do," he said as he nodded to Bunch to pour him another shot of good whiskey.

CHAPTER SEVENTEEN

It was late in the afternoon and Elam Roper was still in his long johns. His pistol was on the table and he was eating some vegetable soup. Several of the other gunmen were sitting around playing cards and drinking. Lester and two other men came riding up to the front of the saloon just as a store owner was sweeping off his porch.

Lester leered at him. "Get your sorry ass back inside!" he hollered. The scrawny man dropped the broom and ran inside, slamming the door.

Lester turned to Saul Rivard. "Remind me to kill him next," he ordered as he headed up the steps and inside the saloon.

Elam looked at his brother scathingly. "Well, did you clear the trail?" he asked Lester, whose face scrunched up with agitation.

"No, some of those damn boulders weigh more than a horse," he answered.

Elam threw his spoon down on the table and wiped his mouth. "Well, we still have three trails out of here if we need to make a run for it," said Rivard as he walked in.

Elam picked up the spoon and threw it at Rivard. "We ain't runnin' from that sumbitch," he said. "We're gonna catch his sorry ass and torture him before we burn him alive on a wooden cross."

"I agree, brother," said Lester as he sat down and poured himself some coffee.

"Do you have guards posted on the roof?" Elam asked Lester.

"Yeah, but they ain't likin' it one bit."

"Tell them to keep their heads down," he said.

"They are, but they're still complaining about it."

"Then go up there and shoot one of them yourself," hollered Elam, loud enough for the man on top of the saloon to hear him.

* * *

Jess and Carmichael slept in rooms across from each other in the Red Creek. Neither trusted the other and each of them propped a chair under the door handle. In the morning, when Jess walked out of his room, the door to Carmichael's room slowly opened. He had his pistol in his hand and a concerned look. Jess smiled at him as he tightened the hammer strap over his own pistol as a show of good faith. Carmichael holstered his pistol with a nervous smile on his face.

They walked downstairs where several men were eating breakfast. The two of them sat down and Bunch delivered them a meal of ham and eggs. They ate in silence, finishing their meals with some more hot coffee. Carmichael set his cup down and leaned back in his chair.

"So, what's the plan, now that we've agreed to work together…for now that is," he said. Jess stuck another piece of ham in his mouth and stared at Carmichael as he finished chewing it. He washed it down with a sip of coffee.

"We're going to slowly kill every man the Ropers have working for them in Hades."

"It's that simple, just kill them one at a time?"

"Maybe two at a time with you helping me."

"So, we're gonna just walk down the street and shoot whoever shows himself?"

"No, we're going to put some more fear into them first."

"Isn't that what they've been doing?"

"Exactly, and we're going to turn it back on them."

"Sounds like you have it all figured out."

"Mostly, but there is a lot more to be done."

"I'm listening."

"Do you know your way around a Sharps buffalo rifle?"

"I used to be a sniper in the Civil War, not that I'm proud of it."

"What side did you fight for?"

"Does it really matter?" He scowled. "Damn war killed most everyone I knew and for what? Nothing has really changed all that much. Maybe in the future it will make a difference. I really don't know. I just did my job and kept my head down."

"How many kills do you have to your name?"

Carmichael lowered his head slightly. "After the tenth one, I quit counting and thinking about it," he admitted. "It never squared with me to shoot a man who never saw it coming or didn't have a chance to defend himself, but that was my orders and I took an oath."

"I suppose I was lucky enough to have been too young at the time," said Jess.

"And yet, here you are, killing wanted men for a living." His face hardened as he thought of his brother lying in the cemetery.

Jess noticed the look in his eyes. "If you want to give me the five hundred back and leave, then do it," he said firmly.

"Maybe I'll give you the five hundred back and then challenge you instead. And after I kill you, I'll take everything you have.

Jess sighed and looked at him harshly. "Listen, I only kill men for two reasons," he explained. "One, is because they're wanted by the law for heinous crimes, like murder, rape and such. The second reason is if a man is trying to kill me. When either of those two things happens, it doesn't matter to me how I get the job done. If they're running and I have to shoot them in the back, I'll not hesitate. I always try to give them a fair fight, but the way I see it, if a man needs killing, it don't really matter how it happens. The end result is the same. I live by my own set of rules and that's how I've stayed alive so far."

"Why are you telling me all this?" queried Carmichael.

"Because if I think you're going to try to kill me, I'll plug you straight on or slit your throat in your sleep if I have to, but you'll end up dead one way or another, unless you get the drop on me and kill me first."

"Not exactly a good way to start a partnership, the way I see it."

"I'm not sure we have a partnership yet the way you're talking."

"And what does that mean?"

"It means I don't rightly trust you yet."

"You don't think I'm a man of my word?" demanded Carmichael. "I told you last night that we had a deal."

"And this morning you came out of your room holding a gun in your hand. A few minutes ago you said you might give me the five hundred back and try to kill me."

"You murdered my only brother, damn it," he said through clenched teeth.

Jess leaned forward in the chair and glared at him. "And if you're planning on doing something about it, let's get it over with now," he said bluntly. "If not, I don't want to hear another word on the matter until we finish with the Ropers and their gang of murderers. I won't say it again. Either stand up and shuck that Colt out and get a dirt blanket or drop it until it's over. Make a choice and make it right now. I don't care which one it is either."

Carmichael's eyes glistened with anger and confliction. He glared back at Jess for a long moment. During that time, no one in the saloon took a breath. Then Carmichael's tension slowly left his body and his eyes took on a look of acceptance. He slowly slid his hand across the table with his palm open. Jess reached over and locked hands with him.

"Do we have a deal…again?" Jess asked.

"Yes, but as I said before, I still reserve the right to brace you straight up when it's over," said Carmichael.

"So I don't have to worry about you shooting me out of the saddle or slitting my throat in the middle of the night?"

Carmichael nodded. "And do I have the same guarantee from you?" he asked.

Jess smiled at him. "Yeah, as long as you don't give me a reason," he said as he cocked his head.

"I guess I can accept that," agreed Carmichael as they shook hands and leaned back in their chairs, listening to everyone exhale.

"Good," said Jess. He looked over at Bunch, who was wiping sweat from his brow.

"Cut Marshal Schneider down and bury him proper," he told Bunch.

"But Elam's men said if they come back and he ain't hanging there, they'll kill two of us and they don't care which two," Bunch argued.

"The Ropers and their men are going to be too busy to bother with this town anymore," Jess told him. "And if they do come back, station some men with rifles and shotguns on the roofs and throw them a lead party when they arrive."

"Okay, I'll do what I can, but most men in town won't fight those killers," he admitted.

"I'll help," said one of the men inside the saloon.

"Me too," said another. "I'm tired of being afraid all the time."

"Count me in," said another.

Jess smiled at Bunch. "Looks like you've got a good start," he said.

"I've got some eight-gauge express shotguns in the general store," added the owner. "They cut a wide swath when you pull the triggers."

Jess looked at Carmichael. "Let's get our things and head out."

The two of them stood up, went to their rooms and retrieved their things. They went to the livery, saddled their horses and made a stop at the general store, where the owner was handing out the eight-gauge shotguns and boxes of shells to go with them to some of the men in town. Jess purchased food supplies and a lot more dynamite, as well as ammunition for all his weapons except for the custom-loaded cartridges for his buffalo rifles, since he had plenty of them. The two of them climbed up in the saddle and headed west out of town along the wide trail leading into Hades.

Carmichael turned to Jess with a strange smile. "I always figured that one day I'd be taking my seat in hell, but I never figured I'd be riding my horse there," he said with the slightest hint of a smile.

Jess smiled back at him. "Actually, I renamed the town Hell."

CHAPTER EIGHTEEN

Jess and Carmichael rode in silence all the way along the wide trail until they came to the remains of the woman Elam's men had burned on the wooden cross.

Carmichael stared at the macabre scene for a long moment. "This is what they've been doing to the townsfolk?" he asked softly.

"Yeah, along with cutting their heads off and sticking them on poles and other stuff to make people think twice before continuing on into town."

Doesn't take any courage to do something like this," observed Carmichael.

Jess nudged Gray into a slow walk farther along the trail until they got close to the sign Jess had pounded in the ground. "This spot is perfect," he said as he slid from the saddle.

He looked at the tall pillars and rocky ledges that lined the trail. He walked to Sharps and started removing some dynamite from the saddlebags. Carmichael walked to the sign and when he passed it, he turned around and read it.

"Damn," he muttered to himself. He walked back to where Jess was busy placing bundles of dynamite at the bottom of the rocky ledges at the narrowest point of the trail.

"What are you doing?" he asked.

"This trail is the only one coming out of Hades that's wide enough for a wagon," he told him. "I'm going to blow it to hell and cover it with boulders. They won't have a way to use a wagon to get supplies in Chilton."

"What about the innocent people left in Hades?" he asked. "They'll run out of supplies too."

"I figure they can survive another several days if the Roper brothers don't kill them all."

"I get your thinking," he admitted.

Jess finished and placed three long fuses on the ground and tied the ends together. "I figure these fuses are long enough to last about a half hour," he explained. "That should give us enough time to get us close to a spot to hide that I found when I scouted this place out. We'll be able to see the town through my spyglass and get their reaction."

"That's it? We just cut off their supply route and watch?"

"No, we have a lot more to do yet," Jess told him as he lit the fuse.

They headed for their horses and both quickly jumped in the saddle with Jess leading the way. Before they made it to the spot Jess had mentioned, the ground shook as the blast blew tons of rock and debris up into the air. They both turned in the saddle and saw the orange ball of fire surrounded by black smoke and dust off in the distance.

"That oughta get their attention," said Carmichael. He followed Jess along a winding trail heading for the spot Jess had told him about.

* * *

The buildings in Hades shook and the windows rattled. Everyone froze where he sat or stood, looking up as if something might come crashing down. Lester was sitting in a rocking chair on the front porch of the saloon and could see the fireball. The two guards on the rooftops saw it too.

Elam came running out of the doorway of the saloon just in time to catch the fireball fading. "What the hell is happening now?" he whined.

"I don't know, brother, but I'm going to find out," replied Lester. He waved at Rivard who was standing on the front edge of the roof on the building across the street from the saloon.

"Rivard, you're with me," he ordered as he picked up his rifle and went to get a horse. Rivard climbed down from the roof and headed for the livery.

They rode out to the trail where the explosion had taken place. The sign Jess had pounded in was on their side of the explosion and the woman hanging from the wooden cross was on the other side, where the trail was still wide enough for a wagon.

"I don't like this," muttered Rivard. "We have no way of taking a wagon to Chilton for supplies."

"We can still go there by horseback," said Lester as he looked around at all the rubble.

"Do you think the people in Chilton did this to keep us away?"

Lester swung his head around to him. "Naw, those people are afraid of their own shadow," he said. "My guess is it was that bounty hunter who did this."

"But why? What would be the point?"

"I don't know for sure. But something tells me we're gonna find out soon."

"If it was him, do you think he's watching us right now?" asked Rivard, feeling edgy as he nervously looked around.

"No."

"Why do you think that?"

"Because one of us ain't been shot out of the saddle yet," advised Lester. "Let's go and tell Elam what we done seen."

By the time Lester and Rivard got back to Hades, Jess and Carmichael were sitting in the spot Jess had found that provided them good cover and a view of the town. When Jess saw them riding back in, he extended the spyglass and watched them. Lester and Rivard walked inside the saloon to find Elam with his boots stuck up on a table. He was leaning back in a chair cleaning his fingernails with a pocketknife.

"Well?" asked Elam.

"Boss, someone blew up the ledges by the wide trail heading to Chilton," Rivard told him as Lester busied himself with pouring some whiskey.

Elam jerked his feet off the table and leaned forward in the chair. "Someone, my ass," he hissed through thin lips. "It was that damn bounty hunter who did it."

"We don't know that for certain," argued Lester after downing a shot of whiskey.

"Who else could it be?" asked Elam. "And why haven't you done anything to stop him yet?"

"I thought you were the boss of this outfit," said Lester with a scowl. "Why don't you figure something out?"

"Just go out there, find him and bring him to me," ordered Elam.

"We haven't even seen him and if we send men out to find him, we leave the town shorthanded. He has dozens of places to pick us off from around the town," said Lester. "That's why we picked this town in the first place. It's hard to move around out there and someone who is smart enough can use that to his advantage. He's already picked off two of our guards on the roofs, killed Stumpy while he was taking a piss and then blew one of our men to pieces the other day. I say we either hunker down here until he shows himself or find another place to hole up."

Elam pounded his fist on the table. "I done told you, he ain't runnin' us out," he spat angrily.

"Then you come up with another plan," Lester said as he poured himself more whiskey.

Elam turned to Rivard. "Get the guards off the roofs and have them stay inside until we figure out something," he told him.

Rivard nodded and headed outside to tell the guards, whispering to himself. "First smart thing we've done so far."

* * *

Jess and Carmichael were still at their hiding spot. Their horses were hidden from view and they were at a distance that even a buffalo rifle couldn't reach any of the men in town. Jess watched through his spyglass when the guards on the rooftops were told to come down and go inside.

"What's happening?" asked Carmichael.

"After they came back, they removed the guards from the rooftops," Jess told him as he handed the spyglass to him. Carmichael looked through it and saw no guards anywhere. He handed the spyglass back to Jess.

"Why do you think they did that?"

"I already picked off a few of them the other day. I guess they don't want to give me another chance."

Carmichael handed the spyglass back to Jess. "So, what do we do now, just sit and wait?"

"No, we're going down there tonight and plant some dynamite."

"We are?" he asked.

"Yeah."

"And then what?"

"Actually, before that, I'm going to show you the spot you'll be shooting from over there," he said pointing.

He looked over at the area Jess was showing him and frowned. "I ain't hitting anyone with my Winchester from that distance."

"You'll be using one of my Sharps rifles with some custom-loaded cartridges."

"Custom-loaded cartridges?"

"Yeah," he said as he pulled one from his pocket and showed it to him.

Carmichael examined the round and felt the weight in his hand. "It feels a little lighter."

"The slug is three hundred seventy-five grains and has about ten percent more gunpowder inside," explained Jess. "They shoot flatter and longer than the factory loads."

Carmichael smiled slightly. "I wish I'd had these during the Civil War, but they probably wouldn't have worked in the rifles we had available back then."

"Let's get you the rifle and a dozen rounds and move your horse over to that other spot in case we have to make a run for it."

Carmichael looked around behind them and frowned. "Run to where?" he asked dubiously.

"Don't worry. I'll show you the way out of here. I spent some time clearing a pathway that will get us to the flatland if we have to retreat."

"All right, but where are we going to bury the dynamite down there?"

"I see several places to bury it." Jess pointed. "One there, one there and a few of them on the trails leading up here in case they see us."

"Just how many men do they have left down there?"

"I don't know for certain, since they mostly stay inside except for when one of them comes out to piss or use the outhouse."

Carmichael smiled slightly at that. "Maybe we should plant one stick behind that," he said. "Wouldn't that be one hell of a surprise?"

"I like the way you think," Jess told him.

CHAPTER NINETEEN

Jess and Carmichael ate a cold meal with no coffee for fear of the fire being seen by someone in town. After that, they both took naps as they waited for the middle of the night to arrive. Jess woke and went to nudge Carmichael, but he was moaning softly as his sweaty head moved back and forth. Jess saw his pistol on his lap and before nudging him to wake, he put his left hand on it.

"Hey, wake up," he whispered. Carmichael jolted awake trying to raise his pistol, but found a hand holding it.

"Take the shot…take the shot…" muttered Carmichael in a daze.

"The war's over with," Jess told him. Carmichael got his bearings and relaxed. Jess let go of the pistol.

"I was worried you were going to shoot me," Jess told him.

Carmichael wiped his forehead and sighed loudly. "Damn nightmares," he cursed quietly. "I fight that war over again almost every night in my head."

"Save it for tomorrow, because that's when the war really starts," Jess told him.

"I gotta have coffee."

"We can't chance it. Besides, we have a lot of work to do before daylight."

"Okay," he said as he put his hat on and holstered his pistol.

The two of them packed a bag with dynamite, fuses and some rocks. Jess slung the sack over his shoulder. They slowly made their way down the steep hill, each with a small shovel in one hand and a rifle in the other. When they reached the bottom, they took a minute to look around. The place was silent, with only a slight breeze moving through the town.

Jess pointed to the west end of town. "Here, bury two sticks of dynamite far enough not to damage the buildings at that end and put the rocks on top of the dynamite," he explained. "I'll do the same on the east end. Then, we'll meet back here and figure out what to do next."

Carmichael nodded and headed for the west end, staying in the shadows whenever possible. When they were done, they met back up. They both stiffened when they saw a light getting brighter near the back of the saloon. They got on their stomachs and waited. One of Elam's men came walking out the back of the saloon yawning and holding the oil lamp. He slowly stumbled to the privy out back. He went inside and closed the door, lighting up the privy with the lamp.

"You said you wanted to scare Roper and his men?" whispered Carmichael as he took one stick of dynamite and a handful of rocks that he stuck into his back pockets.

"Yeah."

"I have an idea," he said. "Cover me."

"All right," Jess agreed as he picked his rifle off the ground.

Carmichael stealthily made his way to the privy. Jess was surprised at how silent he was, but he figured it was his experience from his time in the war. He made it to the privy and stood by the side of it. He slid a bowie knife out and waited. The door slowly opened and when the man stepped out, Carmichael silently stepped behind him, clamped his left hand over the man's mouth and cut his throat from ear to ear, making sure he cut both carotid arteries when he did. The lamp fell and broke. Carmichael held the struggling man while using his foot to kick dirt on the lamp, extinguishing the small fire that had started.

The man stopped struggling and became limp. Carmichael slowly let him down to the ground on his back. He used his bowie knife to cut the man's shirt open, exposing his chest. He carved something on the man's chest and then he used the tip of his knife to cut the eyeballs out of the man's head. He used the tip of the knife to throw the eyes behind the privy, knowing the critters would dispose of them before daylight when the body would be discovered. He walked behind the privy and used his knife to bury the stick of dynamite and covered it with the rocks. When he finished, he ran back to where Jess was waiting. Jess was surprised at how quiet he was as he did.

"That should put some more fear into them," Carmichael said.

"What did you carve on that man's chest?"

"Gone to hell," he replied.

"Seems like being a sniper in the war wasn't the only thing you learned."

"I learned a hundred ways to kill or torture a man for information."

"I'm sorry about that, but it looks like it's going to come in handy in this fight," said Jess.

"Yeah, now what?" he asked, avoiding the comment.

Jess looked at the base of the hill. "See those two trails leading up to where we'll be tomorrow?"

"Yeah."

"Let's bury a stick of dynamite on each trail about a hundred feet up the hill. That way, if they do come after us, we can blow the dynamite with the buffalo rifles and hopefully the falling boulders and rock will trample them."

"I'll take that trail over there," said Carmichael, pointing to the spot.

They finished burying the dynamite along the skinny trails and then Jess headed back to the spot where he would stay. Carmichael took his horse and walked him slowly to the spot Jess had shown him where he would be able to shoot at an angle coming from the west end of the town. He hid his horse, took the buffalo rifle and sat down, taking out a piece of jerky. He looked up at the eastern horizon and saw the faintest hint of daylight coming.

Jess sat up and waited. As the first rays of daylight turned the dark into shades of gray, he looked over at Carmichael, who was looking back at him. They nodded to one another and then lowered their heads and pushed the buffalo rifles out between the rocks they had put in place.

The saloon slowly came awake in the dawn hours. Elam and Lester were both still sleeping it off in their rooms. Rivard, Powell and Winslow were eating breakfast. Jackknife Savage, a half-breed Cherokee that the Ropers kept around for his tracking and knife skills, was sitting in a corner by himself.

Winslow finished his meal and quickly stood up. "I gotta shit," he said as he headed for the back door. He pushed it open and on his way to the privy he saw the body on the ground.

"What the hell…?" he whispered as he slowly walked closer.

He saw the dead body with the shirt cut open. He saw the bloody letters carved on the chest and a lump formed in his throat, preventing him from calling out. Winslow began walking backward toward the saloon until he bumped into Rivard, who was coming out. Winslow jumped and spun around, his eyes wide with fear.

"What's the matter, Winslow?" asked Rivard. "Did you see a ghost or something?" Winslow didn't speak; he simply pointed a shaky finger toward the dead body.

Rivard looked in that direction and immediately walked around Winslow toward the body. "Elam, Lester, you'd better get out here," he hollered back to the saloon. Elam was snoring and didn't hear it, but Lester was sitting up in bed rubbing his eyes.

"Now what?" Lester said as he walked to the window and looked out. He saw Rivard standing over a dead body outside the privy. He leaned his head out the open window.

"Who is it?" he asked.

"It's Thompson and his throat has been cut," Rivard hollered back. "He's got a message carved on his chest."

"What does it say?"

Rivard turned and looked up at Lester. "It says, 'gone to hell.' "

"Damn it," cursed Lester as he hung his head.

"There's something else too," cautioned Rivard.

"What?"

"Both of his eyes are plucked out."

"Who the hell would do that?" asked Lester in a strained voice.

"The devil," said Winslow from below the window.

"Shut the hell up, Winslow, before I shoot you myself," barked Lester as he pulled his head back in from the window.

Elam came stumbling out of his room, still drunk from the night before. "What the hell is all the screaming about?" he complained.

"Thompson is dead out by the privy," Lester told him.

"I didn't hear no gunshot."

"His throat was slit and the words, 'gone to hell,' are carved on his chest."

"Anyone see anything?"

"No, but someone or something plucked his eyeballs out too," bellowed Lester.

"Probably a vulture," said Elam. "Speaking of the privy, I need to use it." Elam headed down the steps in his long johns again. When he reached the bottom of the steps, he saw Jackknife Savage sharpening his long knife with a stone. He gave him a suspicious gaze.

"Jackknife, did you carve up Thompson?" Jackknife shook his head, his long black hair waving back and forth.

"You said you'd cut his tongue out one day."

"His tongue ain't cut out," said Jackknife as he smiled, exposing his perfect white teeth.

Elam waved his hands in the air and grunted as he headed for the back door of the saloon. Rivard and Winslow were dragging Thompson's body away. Elam walked out and looked up at the hills before heading for the privy. Jess took careful aim at the rocks piled on the stick of dynamite behind the privy. He slowly squeezed back on the trigger. Winslow saw Elam walking to the privy and dropped Thompson's leg.

"I wouldn't go in there if I were you," Winslow called out to him.

Elam spun around and walked toward Winslow to yell at him, but before the words got out of his mouth, the custom-loaded slug hit the rocks and sparks flew. The stick of dynamite exploded, shattering the privy into a millions pieces of wood. Elam felt lumps of urine-soaked crap falling on him as he stood there holding his hands on his head. He wiped his eyes off and turned to see a large hole where the privy once stood. He looked up to the hill as he wiped his face off with his hands.

"You crazy bastard," he screamed at the top of his lungs. "You're gonna regret ever finding us or this town."

He started to turn back toward the saloon when another of the custom-loaded slugs tore through his left shoulder, spinning him around in a circle and knocking him down on the ground. Winslow and Rivard ran to him, picked him up and hauled him into the saloon just as another heavy-caliber slug hit the doorframe, chipping off splinters of wood. They were moving so quickly, Winslow lost his footing and all three of them went down in a heap. Winslow was trying to stand up when a slug crashed into his ankle. He screamed like a banshee and scooted himself inward from the doorway. Rivard grabbed Elam, rolled him

ROBERT J. THOMAS

over himself and threw him farther past the door opening as yet another slug slammed into the floor between his legs. He crawled over Elam for cover, smelling the urine and crap that covered him.

"Son of a bitch," wailed Winslow. "The devil done came to take the town back!"

CHAPTER TWENTY

"That ain't no devil!" yelled Elam. "It's that bounty hunter!"

"Then how do you explain the carving on Thompson?" asked Winslow.

"That bounty hunter cut him with a knife to try to scare us," argued Elam, looking around for a towel to put on his wound.

"Both of his eyes were cut out too," wailed Winslow.

"It was probably vultures," claimed Elam as he wiped his face with his hands.

"But they don't usually feed at night."

Elam stopped wiping his face and glared at him. "Damn it, Winslow, I'm telling you for the last time, this town ain't really haunted!" He screamed as two more slugs slammed into the doorway and the outside wall of the saloon.

"See?" said Elam. "Why would the devil use bullets when he could just pull the entire town down to hell if he wanted to?"

"Maybe he don't want the town, just us," Winslow said with his face still scrunched up in fear.

Elam was about ready to respond, but he didn't. He knew the look on Winslow's face was adamant and nothing he could say would change his mind. He turned to Rivard who was peering around a small window in back.

"Do you see anything?" asked Elam as he shoved a towel into his long johns to help soak up the blood from his shoulder wound.

"I can faintly see smoke coming from two directions, but nothing else," replied Rivard.

"Two places?"

"Yeah, high on those rocky ledges and a good several hundred yards apart."

"So, the bounty hunter has help?"

"It would appear so."

"Let's get into the main room of the saloon," ordered Elam. Winslow finally stood up and limped past the door opening when another slug punctured a hole through his left side, knocking him against the wall. He slowly slid down the wall, the fear screaming in his eyes.

"The devil done claimed my soul!" were the last words he spoke on this side of the living. Elam looked back at him and frowned.

"I was tired of listening to him anyway," said Elam as he flinched from the pain in his shoulder.

Rivard took a quick look at it. "It looks like a clean through and through," Rivard said.

Lester and the other men were hunkered down behind tables and the bar inside when Rivard and Elam walked in from the back. The barkeep, Blake Archer, handed him some warm, wet bar towels to wipe himself off.

Lester looked as nervous as a whore in church. "Brother, I say we leave this hellhole and head to another hideout," he told Elam.

"And I'm telling you for the last time, we ain't leaving!" Elam hollered back. "Now, take some men and go up to where the shots are coming from and kill whoever is up there."

"I thought you wanted to bring him back so you could torture him," argued Lester.

"Well, I've changed my mind. Now I just want him and whoever else is helping him to die," groused Elam as he wiped his face with a warm towel. Lester pointed to four men including Rivard to go with him. The shooting had stopped for now and they made their way to the livery.

Rivard glanced over at Lester with a cautionary look. "Lester, I don't think this is a good idea, riding up those hills," he told him. "We're gonna get picked off by those shooters."

Lester snapped his head around to him. "Don't you think I already know that?" he demanded. "Elam is the boss and we have to do what he says. There can only be one boss of an outfit. If we take fire or lose a man, then we'll retreat, but for now, we do as we're told."

Rivard shook his head and frowned, but he shut up. The other three men didn't look very excited about what they were doing either. Campbell Thurber, Knut Blackson and Raymond Osborne were all taking their time saddling their horses.

"Rivard has a point," advised Thurber. "We should go way around that hill and come at it from the backside. Going up the front is dangerous, especially if the two shooters are still there waiting for us."

"And like I told Rivard, Elam is the boss and we do what we're told," barked Lester stubbornly.

"Well, the last time you went up there after that bounty hunter, one of our men got blown to hell and the other one got shot," added Osborne.

"If you don't want to follow orders, go and tell Elam to his face that you're quitting this outfit and see what happens," dared Lester.

All the men shut up and finished saddling their horses, knowing that confronting Elam meant getting a bullet for their efforts. They climbed up in the saddle and Lester gave each of them one last serious look.

"Now, we take it slowly. Make sure your rifles are cocked and ready at a moment's notice," he told them.

The five of them rode out of the livery, headed around the east end of town and turned toward the rocky hillside where Jess and Carmichael were sitting patiently. Jess waved at Carmichael, but he was already looking at the five men and aiming at the bundle of dynamite buried about twenty yards from them. Carmichael glanced over at him and Jess gave him a thumbs-down signal, letting him know not to blow the dynamite yet. Carmichael understood that he wanted the five men to feel more comfortable and get them to come up the two trails on the hillside, closer to the dynamite.

The two of them waited and watched, pulling the rifle barrels back out of sight and keeping their heads low. The five men below all sat atop their horses waiting to see if they would draw any fire.

After a few minutes, Rivard turned to Lester. "Maybe they took off again," he said.

"Maybe," muttered Lester. "I just don't trust that sumbitch one bit."

Osborne removed his hat and wiped his brow. "How the hell did he blow up the privy when he was up there?" he asked.

"There was a gunshot when it happened," declared Thurber.

"Who could hit a stick of dynamite from that distance?" asked Osborne.

"That don't matter now," said Lester. "Rivard, you and Osborne are with me and we take the trail on the right. Thurber and Blackson, you two take the trail on the left and be extra careful."

"You don't have to tell us that," said Blackson with a hint of sarcasm. Lester caught it, but said nothing since he was feeling just as prickly over the whole idea.

Jess and Carmichael kept exchanging glances as the five men split up and headed for the two trails. Three headed for the one leading close to where Jess was and two headed for the one toward Carmichael. The five men moved slowly and cautiously. When they started climbing the winding trail up the hill, Jess and Carmichael waited until they got fairly close to where the dynamite was buried. Carmichael fired first. The slug smashed into the small pile of rocks covering the dynamite and it exploded, throwing rocks, boulders and debris in the air. Thurber and Blackson's horses reared up as the boulders and debris started sliding down the hillside.

The next second, Jess fired at the dynamite on the trail heading his way. The dynamite boomed and several of the pillars and ledges fell apart from the blast and started down the hillside toward the men. Horses squealed and bucked, trying to get away from the impending landslide.

Thurber and Blackson turned their horses and started down the hill. A large boulder slammed into Thurber's horse, knocking him forward as Thurber slid off the saddle.

His horse kept running down the hillside. When Thurber stood up and started to run, he heard the rumble behind him and turned just in time to have a boulder the size of a horse roll over him. He was dead before the boulder uncovered his feet, which were crushed now.

Blackson finally hit the bottom of the hill and spurred his skittish horse hard, but the heavy-caliber slug ripped through his back, punching out his chest. He slid from the saddle and his foot caught in the stirrup. His horse kept going, the rear hooves smashing into his face.

On the trail leading to Jess, Osborn was in the lead. He jumped from the saddle in an attempt to run sideways, trying to avoid the heavy rocks and debris coming down the hill. One rock the size of a watermelon removed his head cleanly. His headless body stumbled a few feet before it fell to the ground. The debris covered him completely, making the spot his grave in short order.

Lester and Rivard were riding down the trail, Rivard's horse right on the rear of Lester's. When they hit the bottom, Rivard's hat flew off his head as he felt the heat from the heavy-caliber slug on the top of his head. He reached up and felt for blood.

"Son of a bitch!" he hollered as he was pelted with clumps of dirt and small rocks.

Lester and Rivard were making the turn at the one end of town when Jess aimed and fired at the buried dynamite next to the trail. It ignited, throwing dirt up in the air. Both of their horses reared up. Rivard and Lester fell from their saddles and scrambled to stand up. Two slugs spat up dirt next to them as they did. They were running for the cover of the livery when they heard another explosion at the other end of town. When they reached the front of the livery, they saw the fireball fading leaving dirt and debris in the air.

Boulders started slamming into the backs of the buildings on the side of the hill Jess and Carmichael were firing from. Several windows in the buildings shattered and the whole town was trembling. Townsfolk were under tables shaking with fear. Elam and the other men inside the saloon had their guns drawn, but there was nothing to shoot at. Blake Archer sat behind the bar holding a wooden serving tray over his head, his eyes closed tightly and prayers coming from his lips.

Then, a few seconds later, after the last of the debris fell and the last rock hit the back of the buildings, the town became extremely silent. The ground stopped shaking and everyone could smell the acrid odor of the ignited dynamite. Elam was sitting under a table with another man. He still held the towel on his shoulder wound, which was becoming more painful by the second. Rivard and Lester came running into the saloon.

"Son of a bitch! It's like a war out there," yelled Lester. "We lost three men!"

"I heard four explosions," wailed Elam from under the table as Lester knelt down in front of him.

"Yeah, they knew what we would do," said Lester. "They blew dynamite on the trails leading up to them and then they blew dynamite at both ends of the town."

"I can see why they'd blow the trails, but why blow up dirt at both ends of town?" asked a shaken Elam.

"I think they did it to scare the wits out of everybody," replied Lester.

"Well it's damn sure working," complained one of the men in the saloon. Elam finally weakened from loss of blood and started falling backward. Lester grabbed his head and lowered him to the floor.

"Someone go and get the doctor in town," screamed Lester.

"We ain't got no doctor," yelled Archer from behind the bar.

"Damn it," cursed Lester.

CHAPTER TWENTY-ONE

"What do you mean you ain't got no doctor?" demanded Lester.

"Well, we did, before you killed him and cut his head off to stick on a pole outside of town," explained Archer.

"How about one of them people who help a doctor?"

"You shot her and burned her on one of them wooden crosses."

"Someone in this town better know how to tend to a wound."

"I can help some," said Archer. "I used to help the wounded during the Civil War when I was injured myself. I learned a few things."

"Then get your ass out from behind that bar and tend to my brother," ordered Lester.

Archer stood up and put the wooden serving tray on the bar. He walked over to where Elam was and smelled all the urine and crap on him. "Okay, push two tables together and put him on them," he ordered. "Someone start boiling water. One of you go to the general store and get me some chloroform and laudanum."

The men lifted Elam's body and placed it on the tables that the other men had pushed together. One went into the back kitchen area and two of them ran to the general store.

Archer used a knife to cut open Elam's long johns. He was wiping off the wound when Elam moaned and started to wake up.

"What the hell are you doing to me?" demanded Elam.

"You've been shot, brother," said Lester. "Archer here is gonna patch you up."

"He ain't no doctor," moaned Elam.

"We done kilt the doctor in town," said Lester.

"It hurts something awful," wailed Elam. "Did you get the sumbitches who shot me?"

"No, they blew half the hillside up," said Lester. "We lost Thurber, Blackson, Osborne and Winslow." The men who went to the general store came back in with laudanum and chloroform. Archer lifted Elam's head and had him take a few swallows of the stuff. It didn't take long for it to start taking effect.

"I feel better now," said Elam, slurring.

Archer took the bottle of chloroform and poured some on a towel. He motioned for a few men to hold Elam down. He placed the towel over Elam's nose and mouth. He struggled for a few moments before he became limp.

"All right, get the hot towels and a bottle of good whiskey," said Archer as he began to clean the wound off with a whiskey-soaked towel.

He took the time to clean Elam's entire upper body before he started working on the wound. He poured some of the whiskey into the wound and let it soak in until it came out the other side. Elam moaned, but he didn't wake. Archer kept pouring the whiskey in a little at a time, trying to clean and disinfect the wound as best he could.

He looked up at Lester nervously. "I need some gunpowder," he said.

"For what?" demanded Lester.

"I need to cauterize that wound or it'll keep bleeding until he bleeds out. Pull some lead from some bullets or open some shotgun shells to get it."

Lester nodded to the men in the saloon, who started pulling slugs out of their bullets and dumping the gunpowder out. When they had enough, Archer put the gunpowder on a small piece of paper. He poured some more whiskey into the wound and then told the men to get ready to roll Elam onto his side and hold him steady.

"When I light this, he's gonna wake for sure," warned Archer.

He poured the gunpowder into the wound channel and used his baby finger to push it as deep as he could. Then, he poured a small amount of whiskey into the wound to help the gunpowder move farther in.

"Roll him on his side and hold onto him," said Archer as he struck a match to the gunpowder and whiskey.

It flashed brightly and the flames flew from both sides of his wound. His eyes flew open and he squealed in pain. The smell of burned flesh and gunpowder filled the air with a nauseating odor. Elam passed out again and they rolled him onto his back. Archer began crudely stitching both sides of the wound. He wrapped bandage material tightly around his chest and tied it.

When he finished, he looked at Lester. "That's going to last a few days at best, but if you don't get him to a doctor soon, he'll die for certain," he told him.

ROBERT J. THOMAS

"But you said the town don't have a doctor," said Lester.

"No, but there's one in Grover about ten miles east of here." Lester plopped down into a chair and picked up the bottle of whiskey. He took a few long pulls from it, thinking. He looked over at Rivard.

"If me and you take him to Grover, how many men will be left to guard the town?" he asked him.

"Six, maybe seven," he said, unsure at the moment.

"Then we let him rest tonight and leave in the morning to take him to the doctor in Grover," ordered Lester.

"Are you crazy?" demanded Rivard. "That bounty hunter and whoever is helping him will pick us off before we get out of town. Not to mention the fact that we don't know where they might have planted more dynamite out there."

"I know, but I have an idea," said Lester as a vicious smile crossed his lips.

* * *

Jess and Carmichael both stayed in their spots, waiting for anyone else to come up the hill to get them, but no one did. They were watching the rear of the saloon when Jess saw two men run into the general store and come out holding some things in their hands, but he didn't have a clean shot at either of them. After a while, Jess motioned for Carmichael to come back over to his position. It took him a few minutes to walk his horse to where Jess's horses were. He crouched down low as he made his way to where Jess was still on his stomach, peering through his spyglass.

He got down on his stomach and looked down at the hole where the privy used to be.

"Sure made a mess of that thing," he chuckled. "Seen anything interesting yet?"

"No, nothing except two men ran across the street to the store for some supplies," he said without removing the spyglass from his eye.

"I think the dynamite has them worried," he said. "They don't know if we have any more planted in the ground or not. We could move to the opposite side tonight and plant some more."

"No, the other side doesn't have the same cover and high ground we have here," said Jess. "We have an escape route and they have no idea if we have more dynamite planted up here."

"So, now what?"

Jess folded the spyglass up and turned to look at Carmichael. "Why don't you ride back to Chilton and get your horse fed and watered. Bring some more food out for us and bring some grain for my horses. They've got to be hungry by now and there ain't nothing for them to feed on up here."

"Okay, I should make it back by dark if I leave right away."

"Be careful," Jess told him.

"Always," he said as he headed for his horse.

"And take the empty canteens from my horses and fill them up at the river below."

"Got it," he called back.

Jess continued to watch the town for the remainder of the day. He walked behind a ledge and made the smallest fire he could to make coffee. He figured Elam's men knew he was still up here, since they were keeping out of sight. He ate cold beans and peaches and he was getting hungry for a good hot meal. He hoped that Carmichael would make it back safely before dark so they could take turns at watch.

Back in the saloon, Elam slept on the two tables. Lester sat with Rivard and explained his plan for the morning. Rivard agreed it was possible to get Elam out of range from the buffalo rifles by placing innocent townsfolk inside the wagon. The trail heading west turned narrow outside of town, but by then, they could put Elam on his horse and help him stay in the saddle until they reached Grover.

* * *

Zack Bloom and Don Bader were riding their horses along a trail heading to Chilton, their last stop for supplies and whiskey before riding to Hades to join up with the Roper gang. They had ridden in silence for the last few hours.

"So, tell me how much we got from robbin' that bank," said Bader.

Bloom turned his head and smiled at him. "Thirty thousand dollars," he told him again.

"I just like hearing it over and over," acknowledged Bader.

"It's a lot of money, but we'll make even more after joining up with Elam and Lester," said Bloom. "I heard he's gathered a few dozen hard cases or more. We can hit several more banks and trains and collect a lot of cash, gold and silver. Enough to retire on maybe."

"Who says I'm ready to retire?" asked Bader.

"You ain't gettin' any younger," said Bloom.

"When's the last time you looked in a mirror?"

"I ain't much older than you," he argued.

"Yeah, you keep believing that," cackled Bader.

"We should hit Chilton in an hour or so," advised Bloom.

"Good, cause I'm thirsty."

"You're always thirsty."

CHAPTER TWENTY-TWO

Carmichael made his way down the back side of the hill. He stopped at the river and filled up four canteens. He headed for Chilton and when he rode into town, the livery worker was sitting on an overturned wooden box just inside the large doors. He had a nervous look on his face. Carmichael slid from the saddle and handed the reins to the worker, who slowly stood up.

"You might want to turn back around and get out of town," he told Carmichael.

"Why is that?"

"Two men rode in an hour ago and they've been braggin' on how they're going to meet up with the Roper gang in Hades."

"Is that so?"

"I heard it myself."

"Well, feed and water my horse and get me a bag of grain to take with me," he told him as he slipped his hammer strap off and spun on his heels.

He walked out of the livery and looked down at the Red Creek Saloon. Two horses were tied to the hitch rail in front of it. He looked around town and didn't see anyone else out on the street. He stood there for a long moment, wondering if he should go to the general store and get the things he needed or go to the saloon and talk to the two men who were going to join the Ropers. If they joined them, he and Jess would have two more men to run out or kill, and the latter was more likely.

Without thinking or realizing it, his feet started moving toward the saloon as if they had minds of their own. He pictured himself in his uniform leading a charge against the enemy and all the blood and gore that followed. He heard the final screams and wails of pain in his head as men died on the battlefield as clear as if he were there right now.

Sweat began dripping down his cheeks, but his feet kept moving ahead like soldiers in battle following orders, never stopping until he was standing outside the batwing doors of the saloon. It was only then that he saw Tom Bunch standing behind the bar and shaking his head with a worried look on his face. He reached down to remove the hammer strap from his Colt, but somehow, it was already off.

He saw the two men standing at the bar drinking from a bottle of rye whiskey. One of them glanced at him, but turned back around, dismissing him for a local. His hearing seemed off, as if he had fingers stuck in them. He heard things, but they sounded hollow and dim. The dying screams faded away as his hearing seemed to slowly come back to him. One drop of sweat dangled on the tip of his nose and he watched it drop and fall onto the boardwalk. When it hit, it sounded like a cannon shot, and that's when all his senses seemed to come back to him. He went through the batwings and up to the bar. Tom Bunch walked over with a towel and handed it to him. He wiped his face off as his lip quivered, the scar on his face curling up strangely.

"Are you okay?" asked Bunch.

He didn't respond right away. He finished with the towel and handed it back to Bunch. His eyes slowly looked up at Bunch, who could see the torment in them.

"What's wrong with you?" Bunch asked. "You sick or something?"

Carmichael shook his head slowly. "No, I'm fine," he said. "Pour me a whiskey."

Bunch grabbed a bottle and a glass, pouring some whiskey in it as he nodded ever so slightly toward the two men standing at the bar. Carmichael nodded as if to say he knew. Bunch walked away and Carmichael downed the whiskey in one gulp. His shaking hand poured himself another.

He glanced over at the two men and immediately sized them up. The one closest to him was wearing a Navy Colt in a shabby-looking holster that was tied down. He couldn't see the other man's pistol, but he knew they were both hard cases. He made a mental note of how many bullets were in the bullet loops of both men. He counted thirteen in all, not that he needed to. All that mattered were the bullets in the cylinders of their pistols.

His mind went back to a time in the war when he came upon two enemy soldiers who were out of ammunition. He had taken them by surprise and stood there for a long torturous few minutes deciding whether or not to execute them where they stood. His battle-hardened mind told him to pull the trigger, but something he carried with him from the first day of battle stopped him from doing so.

He later learned that one of those two men killed his friends who had run out of ammunition and were attempting to retreat. He didn't realize it, but it changed something in him. That something he had carried with him from the first day of battle seemed to be missing. After that day, he killed the enemy with no forethought or compunction. It didn't matter if they were armed or retreating, he simply killed as many as he could, in any way that he could.

And now, as he stood there looking at the two men, they looked like enemy soldiers. His hands stopped shaking as he downed the second whiskey, never taking his eyes off the two men, who were laughing and talking to each other. Almost unconsciously, he pulled his pistol out and cocked it. The two men stiffened at the sound and turned to face him standing there. Zack Bloom and Don Bader both forced smiles at him.

Bloom spoke first. "You have a problem, Mister?" he asked.

"Yeah, I heard you boys are going to join up with the Ropers," he replied.

"We are, but that don't explain that," declared Bloom nodding at the cocked pistol in his hand.

"Do you know what the Ropers are doing to the people in Hades?"

"Hell, we don't care what they're doing to them," said Bloom. "They're just people."

"They're burning women on wooden crosses and killing men and sticking their heads on poles," he said harshly.

Bloom squinted his eyes at Carmichael and smiled. "Have we met before?"

"I don't think so."

"Yeah, during the war," said Bloom. "You snuck up on me and my partner one day. We was plumb out of ammunition. We both closed our eyes waiting to get the bullet that would send us to hell, but when we opened our eyes, you were gone."

"That was you?" asked Carmichael.

"Yeah, my friend caught a bullet the next day, but I still remember you as clear as day. Ain't that strange? I can't picture my partner in the war, but I still remember your face as if it were yesterday."

"Well, take a good look, because it's your last," he said menacingly. Bloom and Bader exchanged worried looks.

"But the war is over," said Bloom.

"It will be soon."

"But our guns are still strapped in," complained Bader as he stepped out from the bar.

"And if I let you go, you'll go into Hades and kill innocent people who ain't even armed."

"What if we promise to go somewhere else?" asked Bloom. "We've got enough money to go wherever we want to."

"I should've killed you that day and I'm not making the same mistake again," he said as he fired the first slug that tore through Bloom's chest, knocking him back against Bader, who was attempting to remove his hammer strap.

Bloom hit the floor in a loud thud, his pistol still strapped in his holster. Bader had his hammer strap off and was pulling his pistol out when Carmichael fired a second shot that punched a hole in his forehead, dropping him like a sack of flour. Carmichael, seemingly in a daze with his mind somewhere else, fired a second slug into Bader and another one into Bloom. He stood there while the gun smoke lingered in the air.

The smell reminded him of the war and it took him back to the battlefields again. Bunch called his name, but it was faint and way off in the distance. He pictured him and his brother playing in the river at their old homestead. Other things flashed through his mind, stacks of dead bodies, stepping over dead men in trenches and cannon firing. His mind whirled around with flashes of memories, some good, but mostly bad. Bunch called his name louder and he jerked back to consciousness.

"What?" he asked as he slowly turned to Bunch, who stood there with a stunned look on his face.

"I said are you okay?"

"Yeah, why wouldn't I be?"

"Maybe because you just gunned down two men who couldn't even get their guns out of their holsters."

"They were soldiers; they knew what they enlisted for."

Bunch leaned over the bar at the two dead men and grinned as he shook his head. "Those two ain't wearing any uniforms," he advised.

Carmichael shut his eyes for a few seconds and reopened them. He looked down at the two dead men. "Maybe not, but they needed killing anyway. You heard them. They were going to join up with the Ropers."

Bunched leaned back against the bar and smiled. "Hey, I'm not complaining or passing judgment. You probably did everyone a favor by killing them. They were laughing about how they killed a bank manager and a teller a few weeks ago, so I'm sure they're wanted by the law. You want me to keep the bodies at the undertakers for someone to identify later?"

"I don't care," he said as he replaced the spent shells in his pistol. "Pour me another drink."

Bunch poured him another shot of whiskey and had one of the men run out to get the undertaker. A little later, the undertaker came in with the man who had fetched him.

"Haul them to your shop, but keep them in a box for identification later," Bunch told the undertaker. He and the other man started dragging them out.

Bunch looked out at the horses. "What about their horses?"

"You said they were bragging about robbing a bank?"

"Yeah."

Carmichael walked out and went through their saddle-bags and found a bank bag in each one. He looked inside the bags and calculated they had thirty thousand dollars or so in them. He carried them back inside and set them on the bar.

"Is that the money they took from the bank?"

"I don't know, but it most likely is," said Carmichael.

"What are you gonna do with it?" Bunch asked expectantly.

"Was the town marshal married?"

"Why, yes, he was."

Carmichael reached inside one of the bags and pulled out one thousand dollars. He handed it to Bunch, who had a confused look on his face.

"Give that money to his widow," Carmichael said. "I'm sure there's a reward for this money and she deserves it as much as anyone. If you hear about any bank robberies that happened, let me know when I get back. I'll return the money to the rightful owners if they can claim it proper.

Until then, I'll hang onto it. And if you tell anyone about the money, I'll come back and kill you. Understand?"

Bunch leaned over and saw the two blood pools being slowly sucked into the dry plank boards of the saloon floor. "Yes sir, I understand completely," he said plainly.

CHAPTER TWENTY-THREE

Carmichael left the saloon and headed for the livery to get his horse and the bag of grain. He paid the man and headed for the general store to buy some food supplies, including a small ham. He took some pickled eggs out of a jar and ate them. He walked out and packed his saddlebags and strapped the sack of grain to the back of his saddle. He climbed back up in the saddle and rode out of town as if nothing had happened. Bunch stood outside and watched him.

It took several hours before Carmichael reached the spot where Jess was still waiting. Jess stood behind a ledge with his Winchester in his hands until he knew for sure it was him. Carmichael took care of his horse, untied the sack of grain and fed Jess's two horses. Jess brought him a warm cup of coffee and he gladly accepted it. Jess could see the change in his demeanor.

"Everything go okay in town?" he asked.

Carmichael sipped the coffee and swallowed. "Yeah, it went okay."

"You look different somehow."

"I'm the same man."

"What happened in town?" pushed Jess.

Carmichael looked off in the distance and took another sip of the coffee. "I'm not rightly sure, but I killed two men."

"Who?"

"Don't really know their names. It doesn't matter. They're dead."

"Did they come at you?"

"No, they were just drinking."

"I don't understand," said Jess.

"They were planning on coming out here to join up with the Ropers, so I just shot them."

"You just shot them?"

"Yeah, all's fair in war."

"But there ain't no war going on anymore."

"There was today," said Carmichael as he threw the dregs out of the cup and moved to the front ridge, looking down at Hades. "What's happened while I was gone?"

Jess narrowed his eyes and pursed his lips as he walked up next to him. "Get down low before one of them spots us," he told Carmichael, who looked at him sternly.

"Who cares if they see us?" he said. "They know we're here and they can't reach us with rifle fire. I say we go in tomorrow and kill every last one of them."

Jess felt disconcerted, as if he were talking to someone altogether different. His hand slowly moved down to his pistol.

"I wouldn't do that if I were you," warned Carmichael as the tip of his knife pushed against Jess's backside. "This is war, soldier, and don't forget it."

"I don't know what happened to you back in town, but the war is over with," he said calmly. "And if you don't remove that knife from my back, I'll shoot you in your sleep."

Carmichael's eyes glazed over and his eyes fell to the ground as he removed the knife from Jess's back. "Sorry, soldier, I forgot we're fighting on the same side."

"Are you sure you're okay?" Jess asked him.

"No, but I will be," he said as he stared down at Hades.

Carmichael walked back to their bedrolls, leaned against the ledge and immediately fell off to sleep. Jess watched him for a full five minutes before getting up. He took care of Carmichael's horse and watered Gray and Sharps. They had polished off every bit of the grain.

As darkness fell, he let Carmichael sleep while he kept watch on the town below. It was eerily silent and quiet, with only a few oil lamps lit. The only sounds Jess heard out of the ordinary were the moans coming from Carmichael. When he went to wake Carmichael after midnight, his face was streaked with sweat and his lips kept twitching. Jess reached down and felt for the pistol he kept on his lap. He held it gently as he shook him.

"Huh…what?" moaned Carmichael as his head shook back and forth.

"Wake up. It's your turn at watch," Jess told him.

He opened his eyes slowly. "Did I talk in my sleep?" he asked.

"No, just a lot of moaning and groaning. You're all sweaty," Jess told him. "Are you sure you're going to be all right?"

"Yeah, got any coffee?"

"I've kept it warm over behind that ledge, but it's not hot."

"Go on and get some shut-eye," said Carmichael. "I'll wake you at dawn or if anything happens."

Carmichael walked around the ledge, poured himself a cup of coffee and sat down by the edge of the hill, watching the silent town below. He tried to recall the hazy pictures in his mind when he'd killed the two men back in Chilton. The nightmares and memories of the war had begun to fade from his mind, but now, being in a battle against all odds seemed to bring them all back again. He glanced back at Jess a few times, wondering if he was a help or a hindrance at this point. As daylight made its first appearance, Jess woke and threw the blanket off him, exposing his pistol on his lap. Carmichael saw it and smiled.

"I don't blame you," he said, nodding at the pistol.

"I do that every night, but I gotta admit, I was worried about you," Jess said.

"Old war memories," said Carmichael. "I thought they were behind me, but I guess all this has brought it back."

"Anything going on down there?"

"Nothing so far, so I say we fry up some bacon and some of the ham I brought from town," suggested Carmichael.

"I think that's a great idea," said Jess. "I'll get a small fire going." After a while, Jess brought a skillet with the ham and beans mixed in together. They both dug in and were almost finished when they saw movement in the town.

"Something is happening," said Carmichael.

Jess stopped chewing and looked down. He saw a woman driving a wagon out of the livery and toward the saloon. Then, several more of the townsfolk walked out and climbed up in the wagon, which was close enough to the front of the saloon that Jess could only see half of it.

"What the hell do you think they're doing?" asked Carmichael.

"I shot one of them in the shoulder outside the privy," said Jess. "My guess is it's one of the Roper boys and they're taking him to see a doctor."

"Why do you think it's one of the brothers?" asked Carmichael. "We ain't never seen either of them before."

"If it was any of their men, they'd just let him die, so it has to be either Lester or Elam they're going to transport to the nearest doctor."

"Sons of bitches are using those townsfolk as shields," said Carmichael. "What should we do?"

"Wait and see for now," Jess told him as he kept looking through his spyglass. "The way I figure it, the two brothers won't separate if one of them is wounded."

They watched as a few more townsfolk walked to the wagon. They could only see the one side, so when the men carried Elam to the wagon and put him in it, they couldn't see it. Then, a man, whose hands were tied behind his back, walked into the middle of the street and knelt down. The woman driving the wagon looked up at the ridge where Jess and Carmichael were. She cupped her hands together and yelled up.

"Please, don't shoot or they'll kill my husband," she said as she pointed to the man on his knees in the street. "Please, I beg of you."

Lester slowly walked out in plain view.

"Hey, bounty hunter, if you don't let us drive on out of here, my men will execute that man and then I'll kill his wife," he called out. "If you follow us, I'll leave a trail of dead bodies along the way," yelled Lester as he walked over to the man on his knees. "If you don't believe me, I'll blow his brains out right now to prove my point." Lester drew and cocked his pistol, holding it against the man's head. The woman in the wagon started sobbing as she looked up at the ridge.

"Please, tell him you'll let him pass," she spluttered. "They raped and killed my two daughters already. He's all I have left."

Jess looked at Carmichael and then back down to the woman. "All right, we won't shoot. I give you my word," Jess called back.

"I thought you'd come to your senses," cackled Lester as he released the hammer on his pistol and holstered it.

He walked over and climbed up on his horse. Rivard and Ben Dorathy both climbed in the saddle and the woman turned the wagon around in the street and headed west out of town. Elam Roper sat up in the back of the wagon. One extra saddled horse was tied to the back of it. Jess and Carmichael watched the wagon rumble along until it disappeared from sight in some trees and ledges. The man still knelt in the street and a gunshot rang out, the slug spitting up dirt a few feet from the man.

"I guess they want to make sure we stay put," said Carmichael.

"Where do you think they're taking him?"

"Most likely a town called Grover, about ten miles west of here."

"Well, we could make sure the men down there know we're still up here for the rest of the day. Tomorrow we go to Grover and kill them," said Jess.

"Remember when I asked if we were just gonna walk down the middle of the street and shoot anyone who shows themselves?"

"Yeah, I remember," said Jess.

"You know what? With the Ropers gone, maybe that's just what we should do," he said without emotion.

"Is your mind back in the war again?" Jess asked him bluntly.

"Maybe, but that's a good thing," Carmichael replied as he stared down at the man in the middle of the street.

They stood there for a good three hours, thinking about what to do next when they saw the wagon roll back into town. Before the wagon stopped at the livery, another shot rang out from the saloon. The slug smashed into the man kneeling down in the street, knocking him backward in the dirt, his feet flailing out from underneath him. His wife jumped off the wagon and rushed to him. She held his head in her lap and cried as she watched him die. She looked up at the ridge where she could barely see Jess and Carmichael.

"Please, help us!" was the last thing she said before a slug smacked her between the eyes. She fell lifeless onto her husband's dead body. Jess looked at Carmichael, whose face was scrunched up in a hateful, angry look.

"That does it," said Jess. "We're doing exactly what you asked earlier and to hell with the danger."

"I'm with you," Carmichael said as they headed for their horses.

CHAPTER TWENTY-FOUR

Jess and Carmichael made their way down close to the town. They stopped at a spot where they could see part of the side of the street the saloon was on. Jess studied the town some more and made a few mental notes. The husband and wife still lay dead in the middle of the street, two more innocent victims of the ruthless killers. He tried to estimate how many of Elam's men were left in town. He had already killed quite a few and two of them had gone with the Ropers to Grover to see a doctor.

"How do you want to do this?" asked Carmichael, somewhat impatient.

"I'm thinking about it," said Jess. "I'm trying to figure out how many men they have left in the saloon."

"Why not blow up the saloon with the dynamite we have left?"

"I don't want to be responsible for any other deaths of the townsfolk," Jess said as he looked at the dead couple in the street.

"They were killing these poor people before we showed up. They'll just keep slaughtering them until there ain't one of them left regardless of what we do."

"How do you suggest we proceed?" asked Jess.

Carmichael sat straight in the saddle and looked at Jess with an odd faraway look. "I say we march straight in there and kill anyone who comes out with a gun," he said as plainly as he could.

"You know you're not back in the war, don't you?"

"Maybe halfway, but that might be a good thing." He was almost smiling. "So how many do you think are left inside that saloon?"

"I don't really know, maybe five or six, but there might be some hiding in the other buildings."

"Why would they be hiding in other buildings and not the saloon?"

"There are probably still some women left in town, if you get my meaning," Jess told him perceptively.

"All the more reason to end this now. If they want hell, let's give it to them straight on."

Jess looked up at the sun and it was high in the sky. He turned to Carmichael. "You only have one pistol and one rifle."

"It's all I need," he said confidently. "I never miss what I'm aiming at."

"Okay, but you stay on the right side of the street and I'll take the left," said Jess.

"Fine, let's get this skirmish over with."

They rode their horses closer to the west end of town. They found a spot in some trees where they could leave their horses. They both checked their weapons and walked toward the last piece of cover before partially showing themselves. Carmichael chuckled and Jess swiveled his head back to see him.

"You think this is funny?" he asked.

Carmichael shook his head. "No, I was just thinking. If they kill the both of us, they'll find thirty thousand dollars in my saddlebags. They'll be happy about that."

"Where did you get that much money?"

"I took it off those two I killed back in the saloon in Chilton. I guess they were bragging about robbing a bank somewhere."

"You're just full of surprises," Jess told him as he looked back toward the saloon and saw one man walk just outside the batwings to smoke a cigarette.

"You were a sniper, right?" he asked Carmichael without taking his eyes off the man in town.

"Yep, one of the best, not that I'm proud of it."

"See that man standing just outside the batwings?"

Carmichael stepped around Jess slightly to see better. "Yeah, I could pick him off easily."

"Don't."

"Why not?"

"Because when I wound him, someone will come out to drag his body back inside and that's who I want you to kill."

"Okay, but let's not waste another minute."

Jess levered a round into his Winchester and took aim at the man's hip. He fired and Hubbard Dietrich went down. He bounced off the edge of the doorway and fell to the side of the batwings on his back.

"Boys, I've been hit!" he hollered.

Arthur Edenfeld, the leader of the group of men remaining in town, waved his hands at Gus Hustley. "Go and get him!" he ordered.

Hustley ran out and got on his hands and knees and grabbed Dietrich by his ankles. He started pulling him into the batwings, but the slug from Carmichael's rifle entered one side of his head and exited out the top of his skull. He fell lifeless onto Dietrich, who was screaming in pain. Jess already had another round levered in his rifle and he aimed at Dietrich and fired. The slug entered his right ribcage and ripped a hole straight through his heart. The men in the saloon all ducked down and pulled their pistols.

"I thought they were behind us," wailed Weldon Ready.

"I think the devil done came for us," said Kirby Ehler, who was behind the bar with Amund Lucore.

"They ain't devils, just men," said a shaken Edenfeld.

"I say we get the hell out of here," said Zeno Fielding.

"They'd pick us off like rats if we tried that," said Edenfeld. "We stay in here where we have some cover."

"We've been stayin' in here and our men have still been picked off one by one," groused Fielding.

Jess put his rifle back in the scabbard and pulled his pistol and his left-hand short shotgun. Carmichael pulled his Colt and kept his rifle in his left hand. He swung the rifle upward, jerking his wrist and pushing his arm out, levering another round into it.

"Let's go," he said as he walked out from the cover and straight into the street on the opposite side of the saloon.

Jess looked at him worriedly. "He thinks he's back in the war and marching into battle," he muttered to himself as he walked out and headed to the side of the street the saloon was on.

Carmichael walked in a straight line, his eyes glancing up to the rooftops and over to the saloon. Jess moved back and forth, trying to make himself a harder target. He kept watching the buildings and rooftops on the side of the street Carmichael was on.

Inside the saloon, Fielding finally caught sight of Carmichael, who looked like he had no fear and was simply walking along the street with a rifle in one hand and a pistol in the other.

His mind snapped and he stood up from behind a table. "You want me, Lucifer, here I am, you evil bastard," hollered Fielding as he started firing his pistol through the batwing doors.

Carmichael turned his rifle toward the doors as a slug sizzled past his head and slammed into a wall behind him. He ignored it and started walking straight toward the gunfire. Fielding pushed through the batwing doors and fired again. This time the slug burned a furrow in Carmichael's left arm just above the elbow, but he acted as if he didn't even feel it. He fired his rifle and the slug smashed into Fielding's chest at the same time that a slug from Jess's pistol hit him in his left side. He fell to his death at an angle on top of the dead bodies of Dietrich and Hustley. Carmichael flipped the rifle upward again, levering another round into it.

"We're all gonna die," shouted Ora Warriner.

"Shut the hell up," ordered Edenfeld, as Carmichael fired two more slugs into the saloon, one slamming into a table and one into the wall behind the bar. Jess moved farther out into the street, keeping at least ten feet between himself and Carmichael.

"You okay?" Jess asked as he saw the blood dripping into the dirt.

"Just a little scratch," uttered Carmichael as he fired another slug into the saloon doors. The slug clipped Warriner's left ear.

"To hell with this," yelled Warriner. "If I'm dying, I'm going out throwing lead."

"I'm with you," hollered Lucore as he stood up and started firing his rifle through the batwing doors.

The slug knocked Carmichael's hat off his head and he fired another slug from his rifle, hitting Lucore in his left leg. Warriner and Lucore both pushed through the batwings. Lucore levered another shell into his rifle and Warriner fired his pistol wildly at both Jess and Carmichael. They looked like the dogs from hell coming slowly toward the saloon. One of Warriner's slugs cut through the top of Jess's right arm. The slug passed straight through. He fired one of the barrels of the cut-down shotgun in his left hand. The slugs and buckshot hit both Warriner and Lucore.

Carmichael fired his rifle and put a slug into Warriner's throat and then fired his pistol, punching a hole in Lucore's chest. Both men stumbled in the dirt a few steps before falling dead into the street. Carmichael jerked the rifle up and racked another shell into it. He had a dazed look in his eyes.

"You boys are goin' to hell today and nothing can save you," he said as he kept marching toward the batwing doors like a soldier in battle.

Jess moved closer to the batwings. Slugs began pouring out of the saloon doors and windows. Jess fired the second barrel of his cut-down shotgun and dropped it into the street. He threw his pistol into his left hand as he pulled out his right-hand cut-down from the back of his holster, fully aware of the steady rate of fire coming from Carmichael's rifle and pistol. Another slug tore some flesh from Carmichael's right ankle, but he never wavered or stumbled. Jess fired one barrel of his second cut-down shotgun through one window and then fired the second barrel through the other window before dropping it on the ground.

One of the slugs stuffed in the barrels of his shotgun hit Edenfeld in his left side, knocking him onto the floor behind the table he was firing from. Some of the buckshot peppered Kirby Ehler's face, enraging him. Jess holstered his pistol as a slug nicked his left leg above his knee. He flinched at the pain as he slid his large-bore shotgun out.

Ehler stood up and began firing his rifle as fast as he could. Carmichael fired his rifle and pistol at the same time, knocking Ehler one way and then another. Ehler fell back over an overturned table. That left only Edenfeld and Weldon Ready alive in the saloon, with a terrified Blake Archer who was on his hands and knees behind the bar, praying for it to be over. Jess moved closer to Carmichael as they continued toward the saloon doors.

"Whoever is left inside, your days of killing are over with," hollered Jess as they got closer to the batwings.

Jess moved to the right of the opening and Carmichael moved to the left. They exchanged glances and Jess tapped his large-bore, indicating he'd go in first and fill the place with lead and buckshot. Carmichael nodded and Jess pushed the barrel out in sight of the swinging doors. Two pistol shots followed a second later and before Edenfeld and Ready could finish cocking their hammers back, he jumped through the doors and fired both barrels a split second apart, one to the left of the room and one to the right. The twenty .45-caliber slugs and buckshot that followed the roar of the shot-gun engulfed the room with slugs, buckshot and smoke. Edenfeld took several pieces of buckshot and Ready took a slug in his right hand.

"We surrender!" wailed Ready as Jess put the large-bore down on a table and slicked his pistol out. Carmichael walked in and holstered his pistol. Ready slowly stood up with his hands in the air. Carmichael glared at him ominously.

"There ain't no surrender in this fight, soldier," Carmichael told him as he fired one slug that smacked into his forehead. Ready's head jerked backward and he went down like a sack of flour.

Jess watched Edenfeld trying to crawl into the back of the saloon. "Where do you think you're going?" he asked.

"You can't just execute a wounded and unarmed man," cried Edenfeld.

"Then how do you explain the two people lying dead out in the street?" demanded Jess.

"Elam Roper ordered us to do that," blurted Edenfeld.

"Well, the devil said to collect your soul today and he told me to do this," said Jess. He cocked his pistol as Edenfeld slowly turned his head to stare up at the barrel of Jess's pistol.

"Go to hell, you sumbitch!" spat Edenfeld in defiance, knowing he was done for.

Jess fired and the bullet ripped through Edenfield's throat. He slipped onto his back and quivered a few times before becoming stone still. Carmichael looked at Jess.

The saloon was filled with heavy smoke and the smell of gunpowder. They heard a whimper coming from behind the bar and Jess cocked his pistol and Carmichael racked another shell into his rifle.

"You might as well come out of there," Jess said.

"Don't shoot. I'm just the barkeep of this saloon," hollered Archer, still cowering in the corner behind the bar.

"Then come out with your hands up," ordered Carmichael. Archer slowly appeared with his hands in the air shaking. He walked out from behind the bar wearing no weapon, only a dirty apron.

"Yeah, I remember you from the other day when you took a piss," Jess told him. "Any more of them hiding anywhere?"

Archer looked at the dead bodies and shook his head. "No, you done killed them all, except for the Ropers and the two men who left with them."

"Don't worry. We're going after them next and they won't ever be coming back here," he told him as he reloaded the large-bore and slid it back into his back sling.

"Thank the Lord," said Archer.

"You got any good whiskey left back there?" asked Carmichael.

"Yeah, I have at least one bottle."

"Get it out and start pouring," he said as he and Jess started reloading their weapons.

At the top of the ledge where Jess and Carmichael had been shooting from, Jackknife Savage leered down at the town below, exposing his white teeth as he did. His long black hair waved in the wind. During the firefight, no one had seen him slip out the back door of the saloon. He turned and headed north on foot. He could easily live off the land for days, even without water. He stopped and turned back toward town once more.

"One day you will die, bounty hunter," he said to himself as his eyes simmered with hate.

CHAPTER TWENTY-FIVE

Elam Roper rode in the saddle, with Rivard and Lester riding alongside him to make sure he didn't fall off. The going was slow and they finally reached the town of Grover just before sundown. Ben Dorathy, who had been riding vanguard, had them wait until he rode in behind the town and found the doctor's office. Once he did, he retrieved the other three men and stayed behind the buildings to keep out of view from any law in town.

When they reached the doctor's office, Lester helped his brother out of the saddle. Rivard knocked on the back door and pulled his pistol out before the door opened. A short, skinny man opened the door. He was wearing a long white coat that had blood splatters on it. Rivard pointed the pistol at him.

"You the doctor?" he asked.

"Yes, I'm Dr. Shep Aird, but you don't have to point that gun at me to talk," he said with a hint of disdain in his voice.

"I'll decide on that matter," said Rivard. "We have a patient for you." Aird looked past Rivard and saw Elam standing there holding onto Lester for support. His shirt had both dried and fresh bloodstains on it.

"Bring him in," said the doctor. "It wouldn't be the first time I worked on someone wanted by the law."

"Who said we's wanted?" demanded Rivard.

"Don't take me for a fool," scoffed Aird. "If you want him looked at, quit talking and bring him in."

Rivard opened the screen door and Lester helped Elam into the office. They heard moaning coming from a room as the doctor led them into another room farther down the hall. Elam sat on the metal table and the doctor unbuttoned his shirt. After removing the shirt, he picked up a scalpel and Lester and Rivard both cocked their guns and pointed them at the doctor, who froze stone still.

"Easy with the leg cannons, boys," he said. "I'm just going to cut the bandage off to check the wound."

Rivard and Lester released the hammers on their pistols, but they kept them in their hands down by their sides. Dorathy went to the front of the office to stand guard at the front door. The doctor cut the old bandage off and slowly removed the piece of cloth from the front and back of Elam's shoulder. He examined the stitching and the wound and made some grunting sound as he did.

"How bad is it, Doc?" Elam asked.

"Well, the stitching is messy and would have come undone soon," he said. "I see where the wound was cauterized, probably with gunpowder by the smell I'm picking up, but it's already starting to fester. I'll have to completely clean the wound and restitch it. It's going to hurt like hell though, so I'd suggest knocking him out with some chloroform."

"Do what you have to, but do it quick," ordered Lester as he heard loud moaning coming from the other room. "Who the hell is making all that noise?"

"Oh, that's the marshal's prisoner back there," explained the doctor. "He got shot three times and might not make it. The marshal will be in to check on him later."

Rivard looked at Lester knowingly. Lester took the scalpel from the doctor and picked up a towel. The doctor started to follow him, but Rivard raised the pistol up again with a warning look on his face. Lester walked down the hall until he was outside the room where the prisoner was still moaning loudly. His eyes were closed and his face was pale and streaked with sweat. Lester walked up to him and leaned over as he holstered his pistol.

"Sorry about this, pardner, but you've got to shut the hell up before you draw any attention from someone outside," he said. He cut the carotid artery on the man's neck.

Lester held the man's chest and stuck the towel over his neck, which was pumping blood with each heartbeat. It didn't take long before he quit struggling. Lester let go of him and smiled.

"You probably wouldn't have made it anyway," Lester told him as he shrugged his shoulders indifferently before turning around and going back to the room where Elam was now lying on the table. Lester handed the bloody scalpel to the doctor with a witty smile.

"You won't need to worry about your other patient anymore," he told him.

"What the hell did you do?" demanded the doctor.

"I put him out of his misery."

"You killed him?"

"No, those three bullet holes killed him; he just hadn't passed on yet," said Lester. "I just helped him get to hell sooner."

"You can't do that," scolded the doctor. "I might have been able to save that man."

"Shut up and work on my brother or you'll join your other patient," threatened Lester as he jerked his pistol back out and pointed it at him again. The doctor took the scalpel and put it into a metal container of alcohol to sterilize it.

The doctor got out a rag and chloroform and put it over Elam's mouth. He struggled for a few minutes as Rivard held him down. After he became still, the doctor began working on undoing the stitches. It took him about a half hour to completely clean the wound and restitch it. When he was finished bandaging it, Dorathy called out from the front door.

"Boys, we have another problem. The law dog in town seems to be headed straight this way."

Lester nodded at Rivard, who quickly went to the front office. He peered through the thin curtains and saw a man wearing a star on his shirt heading for the office. Rivard saw the desk and he quickly sat down at it, his gun in his hand.

"Let him open the door and then knock him out," Rivard told Dorathy, who nodded and stood to the side of the door. The marshal walked up, opened the door and stepped inside. When he saw Rivard sitting behind the desk, he smiled.

"Is the doctor still here?" were the last words out of his mouth before Dorathy cracked him on his skull with the butt of his pistol as hard as he could. He fell to the floor and Dorathy quickly closed the door.

"What do we do with him?" asked Dorathy.

"He got a good look at me," said Rivard. "You know what to do."

Dorathy holstered his pistol, knelt down and plunged his knife into the marshal's back, the tip of the blade piercing his heart. He grunted and his legs moved around, but he quickly became still. The blood pool under the marshal spread rapidly. Dorathy wiped the knife off on the marshal's shirt. He turned the sign on the window to "closed" and locked the door.

Rivard looked at the dead marshal and then to Dorathy. "Keep watching the front," he said. "I'm going to check on Elam." Dorathy took up a position by the front window and Rivard walked back to the room where Elam was just coming around.

The doctor was washing the blood off his hands at a small sink. "Was that the marshal I heard come in? Where is he?" he asked.

"Where do you think?" asked Rivard. "We can't leave any witnesses."

The doctor dropped the towel as Rivard holstered his pistol and pulled out a long thin-bladed knife. The doctor backed up until his back hit a wall and Rivard rushed him. He shoved the knife into his stomach, turning the blade a half-turn. He tried to scream, but Rivard clamped his hand over the doctor's mouth. He started sliding down the wall as the life drained out of his eyes until he was sitting upright on the floor, his head slumped to the side. Rivard pulled the knife out, wiped it off on the doctor's coat and stood up.

"Looks like we're done here," said Rivard.

Lester helped Elam sit up and Rivard looked through the medicinal cabinet and found two bottles of laudanum. He shoved them into his pockets and called for Dorathy to come to the back. Lester and Rivard had Elam standing when Dorathy walked in.

"Let's get the hell out of town before someone else shows up," said Lester.

They made their way to the back door. Lester helped Elam up in the saddle. The rest of them mounted up and slowly rode away from the doctor's office until they disappeared in some trees. After riding slowly for a few hours, Elam started slipping off his horse repeatedly. Lester looked over at Rivard, who nodded.

Lester called ahead to Dorathy, who was taking the lead. "Find a place to make camp. Elam has to rest a while."

Dorathy quickly found a suitable spot for a camp that had water and plenty of grass for their horses to feed on. Dorathy took care of the horses, while Lester and Rivard took care of getting Elam into his bedroll with an extra blanket on him. Lester gave him a swallow of the laudanum and he quickly fell off to a fitful sleep, moaning and groaning softly.

After the other men finished a hot meal, Rivard looked over at Lester. "When do we head back to Hades?" he asked.

Lester fidgeted with his coffee cup as he thought about it. "Never," he said plainly. Dorathy and Rivard exchanged confused looks.

"What do you mean never?" asked Rivard.

"Exactly what I said," said Lester. "Listen, we have all the money with us. That town may not have been cursed when we took it over, but it sure is now. That damn bounty hunter and whoever is helping him must have been sent by the devil himself. I say we keep heading west and start forming another gang."

"What does Elam say about it?" asked Dorathy.

"We'll ask him in the morning, but I think he'll agree," said Lester.

"Then let's get some shut-eye and talk in the morning," said Rivard as he looked over at Dorathy. "You take first watch and wake me later. Best to leave Lester to take care of Elam during the night."

Dorathy threw the last of his coffee out of his cup, grabbed his rifle and found a spot to sit on a dead log. Rivard and Lester crawled into their bedrolls. Elam woke several times during the night. Lester gave him a little nip of the laudanum each time and he fell back to sleep quickly.

CHAPTER TWENTY-SIX

Jess and Carmichael were on their second whiskey when an old frail-looking man walked in holding the two short twelve-gauge shotguns in his hands. Jess started to reach for his pistol, but the man quickly put them down on the nearest table.

"I mean no harm," he said. "I just thought you wanted them back."

"Thanks," Jess told him as he moved his right hand away from his pistol. He tucked the two short shotguns into the back of his holster, knowing he'd have to clean and oil them thoroughly before using them. The man was staring at the bottle of whiskey and licking his lips.

"I ain't been able to have a drink in weeks," said the man. "I don't suppose you'd want to let an old geezer imbibe in some of that coffin varnish."

Jess turned to the barkeep. "How much whiskey do you have left back there?" he asked.

Archer turned and took a quick count. "I have a dozen bottles of the cheap stuff."

"Save this bottle of the good stuff for us and hand out the rest to anyone who wants a drink and charge it all to me," he told the barkeep before he turned to the old man.

"Drinks are on us," he told him.

The old man rushed to the bar and grabbed a bottle and a glass. "Thanks, Mister, especially for ridding the town of those murderous thugs," he said as he nodded at the dead bodies.

The old man turned a table and chair upright and sat down. A few more of the local men walked in and Archer had them drag the dead bodies outside. After a while, a dozen or so men were inside drinking and feeling normal for the first time in a very long time.

Archer noticed the blood on both Jess and Carmichael. "You boys took some lead," he said. "Best if you let one of the women left in town tend to your wounds."

"Send for one and she can patch us up right in here," said Carmichael.

Archer waved for one of the men to go and get the woman who assisted the doctor before the Ropers killed him. A while later, a pretty young woman walked in holding a black leather bag. She set the bag down on the table closest to the swinging doors. She looked at both Jess and Carmichael and summed up their injuries quickly.

"Who wants to go first?" she asked. Carmichael smiled at her as he walked over to where she stood.

"How 'bout you take care of me first," he said, grinning. She smiled back at him, took the glass of whiskey from his hand and downed it. After it went down, she shook her head and coughed.

"Okay then, sit down right here," she said.

"I'll sit wherever you say, pretty lady," he drawled like a love-struck school kid, staring at her eyes.

"Is that so?" she asked teasingly.

"Yes, ma'am," he said as he kept staring at her. "You can sit on my lap if you've a mind to."

She looked at him wittily. "What's your name, soldier?" she asked.

"How'd you know I was a soldier?"

"I watched how you marched straight toward possible death. I've seen it before. My late husband fought in the war and I could always see that faraway look in his eyes he'd get when he was back in battle sitting by the fireplace at night. You had that same look. But enough of that; let's get you patched up." She quickly cleaned and bandaged his arm and ankle. When she was done, she handed him his empty glass with an audacious look.

"So, how long are you staying in town, Mr. Soldier?"

"The name is Jason Carmichael. I have to leave to find the other men who left," he told her. "But after that, I can come back and stay as long as you want me to."

She sighed and put her hands on her hips. "You go and finish what you started and come back here and let's see how things go," she told him as she leaned over and kissed him on the cheek. Her index finger gently ran along the scar on his face. "And make sure you take a bath before calling on me. My name is Pearl. Anyone in town can tell you where to find me."

"I'll be back as soon as I can," he told her as he took her hand and kissed it. He stood up and walked back over to the bar, where Jess had been watching it all.

"It looks like you got more than patched up," Jess told him.

Carmichael poured some more whiskey in his glass and sipped it. "I do believe you're right," he chuckled. Jess looked at Pearl, who was wiggling her index finger at him. He made sure to refill his glass before walking over. He handed it to her. She downed it and put the glass on the table.

"And you are?" she asked.

"Name is Jess Williams."

"Really? You're Jess Williams, the bounty hunter?"

"Yeah, you heard of me?"

"My husband read all those dime novels about you over and over again until he passed away last year from some unknown disease."

"I'm sorry about your loss," he told her. She nodded and went to work on his arm and leg. When she finished, she smiled at him.

"That should do," she said.

"Don't I get a kiss on the cheek too?" he asked.

She gave him a clever smile and shook her head. "I'm not wasting my kisses on you," she said as politely as she could. "I can see it in your eyes. You're a long way from stopping what you're doing, hunting men down and killing them. I'm looking for a man who can stay with me forever."

"Okay, but it's just a kiss, and it'll make him jealous, which is what you want, right?" She looked over at Carmichael and then leaned down and kissed Jess on the cheek. Carmichael frowned at them both and she giggled.

"I think it worked," she whispered.

"It did for me," chuckled Jess.

She slapped him on his back. "Get back to the bar, Mr. Williams. I'm done with you, but will you do me a favor?"

"What?"

"Keep that one alive so he can come back here," she said.

"You have no idea what you just asked of me," he told her. "But I'll do my best." Jess picked his glass up and walked back to the bar next to Carmichael, who was still staring at Pearl. She smiled at both of them and walked out carrying the black medicine bag.

Jess turned to Carmichael. "I think she likes you."

"Really?"

"Pretty sure."

"But she kissed you too."

"Not the same."

"What do you mean?"

"She made me promise to try and get you back here safely."

"She did?"

"Yep."

"So, she wants me to come back?"

"Yeah, but I told her it wouldn't be an easy job keeping you alive."

"What do you mean?"

"I saw that look in your eyes as we marched toward this saloon. You might as well have had your old uniform on."

"I suppose so, but when I hear gunshots, my mind wanders back to the battles and skirmishes in the war," admitted Carmichael. "And, I suppose the fact that I didn't have anything to really live for anymore affected my judgment a little."

"A little?" Jess asked with an astonished look on his face.

"Okay, maybe a bit more than a little," he agreed.

Jess took a sip of his whiskey and set it back down with a serious look in his eyes. "Listen, I still have to go and hunt down the Roper brothers and the two men who left with them," he said. "If you want to stay here and see what happens between you and Pearl, I understand completely."

Carmichael bit his lip and shook his head. "No, I agreed to join you in this fight and I'll stay in it to the end. Besides, if we can collect some good bounty money on them, I'll have something to offer Pearl besides an ornery man with a horse and a gun."

"That reminds me. We should go and get our horses where we left them."

"They'll be fine for a few minutes while we celebrate freeing the town," said Carmichael.

"Did you forget?"

"Forget what?"

"Bank bags? Saddlebags?"

"Oh, I did forget. Let's go and get the horses stabled and get rooms upstairs for the night. We can head out in the morning to go after the Roper brothers."

They walked out of the saloon and headed for their horses. Jess looked at the blood pool left from the husband and wife who had been shot dead in the street. Someone had already removed the bodies. Anger welled up inside him.

When they reached their horses, Carmichael checked to make sure the money was still in his saddlebags. They were walking their horses toward the livery when a pudgy man wearing a wrinkled worn-out suit approached them with two other men. Jess and Carmichael stopped and waited. The pudgy man stuck his hand out and smiled.

"I'm the mayor of this town and these two men are council members," he said in an official tone of voice. "We want to thank you for saving our town from ruination. If there is anything we can do for you, anything at all, just tell us."

Jess shook his hand. "As a matter of fact, I know exactly what you can do for us," he said. "Have the men in town clear the trail going to Chilton first. You'll find enough white paint at the general store there to paint the entire town. It's already paid for. When the men go to Chilton, tell anyone there who wants to work to come here and help with the painting and clearing the trails going in and out of town. Oh, and rename the town. This ain't Hades or Hell anymore."

"But, we have no money to hire any help and we don't have many people left in town," said the mayor. Jess pulled out a large wad of money and counted out a thousand dollars. He handed it to the mayor, who looked at the money skeptically.

"I don't know exactly what to say," he stammered as he looked at the two councilmen, who just stood there seemingly dazed and confused.

"Just say you'll get on it right away," Jess told him.

"We will, but what if those other men come back here?" asked the mayor.

"The Roper brothers and the last of their men are going to hell, but they ain't coming here ever again," Jess said with confidence.

"How can you be certain of it?" asked the mayor.

"Because tomorrow morning we're going to hunt them down until every last one of them has taken his rightful seat in hell," said Jess.

"Okay, I'll get started on it right away," agreed the mayor as he and the other two men walked away.

Carmichael watched them for a few seconds and then swiveled his head to Jess. "That was a right nice thing you just did, giving this town a chance at starting over again," he said.

"They've been through more torment than most people face in a lifetime. They deserve to live a somewhat normal life."

"Let's get something to eat, a good night's rest and start out first thing in the morning," said Carmichael.

"I agree," said Jess. "Tomorrow, the Ropers should feel the dogs of hell on their backside."

CHAPTER TWENTY-SEVEN

Elam sat staring at the fire with a blanket wrapped around his shoulders. He held a bottle of laudanum in his hand. He uncorked the bottle and took another sip of it and sighed. Drool dripped down the corner of his mouth and he wiped it with the back of his hand. Lester kept watching him as he made some coffee. When it was finished, he poured a cup of it and handed it to Elam.

"Here, drink this coffee and give me that shit," Lester told him. "That stuff will mess with your head."

Elam took the cup of coffee, but he corked the bottle and stuck in into his front pocket. "It takes the pain away," he said.

"I know that, but you can only take so much of it," argued Lester.

"Shut up and warm up some beans," said Elam. Rivard and Dorathy exchanged worried glances, but they said nothing for fear that Elam would shoot them. Lester handed a plate of beans to Elam, who slowly sat there eating them, still staring at the fire. Rivard cleared his throat and put his coffee cup down.

"Boss, Lester suggested that we don't go back to Hades," he said cautiously. Elam slowly looked up from the fire, looking somewhat confused.

"What's this talk about Hades?" he asked. The three men looked back and forth between each other for a long moment before Lester spoke.

"Don't you remember?" he asked. "The town we took over? The bounty hunter who showed up and started killing our men and blowing up stuff?"

Elam searched his foggy brain and then it came back to him. "Yeah, I remember," he said. "Did we kill him?"

"No, he's still out there somewhere and he has someone helping him," said Lester.

"So, why don't you want to go back to Hades?" asked Elam as he spooned some beans into his mouth, a few of them falling on his lap. Lester looked at Rivard and Dorathy before looking back at Elam.

"Well, we had about a half-dozen men back there when we left and who knows how many more that damn bounty hunter has killed since then," explained Lester. "You're wounded and there ain't no doctor left in Hades. You're gonna need to see another doctor in a few days, so I say we keep riding west and start forming another gang."

Elam finished his beans and threw the tin plate into the fire. "So, we let that bounty hunter beat us?" he growled.

Lester shook his head. "I'm not lookin' at it that way. I'm just saying we should keep you alive and start over. There are lots of small towns we can take over once we get enough men to join us."

Elam looked up at Rivard and Dorathy through bleary unfocused eyes. "And what do you two say?" he asked. Rivard and Dorathy both nodded affirmatively.

"We think it's the best idea right now," admitted Rivard. "Your shoulder wound is pretty bad and you've lost a lot of blood. You won't be back to normal for a while and you'll need more doctoring like Lester said." Lester used his spoon to remove the tin plate from the fire as he listened to Rivard. When he finished, he looked up at Elam, who was uncorking the bottle of laudanum again.

"Quit drinking that stuff," Lester said gruffly.

"It kills the pain," spat Elam as he took a nip and corked the bottle again.

"It's gonna kill you if you keep drinking so much of it," countered Lester.

Elam pulled out his pistol and pointed it at Lester. "How 'bout I shoot you in the shoulder?" asked Elam sarcastically. "Let's see how long it is before you start begging for the bottle."

"Put that gun away before you shoot someone by accident."

"Don't forget who's the boss of this outfit," said Elam as he holstered his pistol. "Now, if we ain't going back to Hades, where are we going?"

"There's a town called Stony Creek about a two-day ride from here at the rate we can travel with you being wounded," said Lester. "We can get you tended to again, resupply and keep heading west looking for men to join us along the way."

Elam pulled the blanket tighter around his shoulders as he shook from the chill of the morning air. "Then clean this up and let's get moving," he ordered as he stared into the dwindling fire. They broke camp and headed west along a little-used trail toward Stony Creek.

* * *

Jess and Carmichael ate, had a few more drinks and then took turns using the bathhouse behind the saloon. After that, they slept in rooms on the second floor, compliments of Archer. Both men were so tired they slept past first light. Jess finally stirred and felt the stiffness in his right arm. He slowly got dressed and washed his face, drying it with a towel on the dresser. He put his guns on and moved his right arm around gently to loosen it up. He put some extra pressure on his leg to check it. It was sore, but it wouldn't slow him down. He opened the door at the same time that Carmichael did. They looked at one another and grinned.

"You look like hell," Jess told him.

"You don't look much better," chuckled Carmichael.

They both caught a whiff of bacon frying and headed down the steps. When they reached the bottom, several men were eating eggs, bacon and ham. The townspeople nodded at them, with thankful looks in their eyes. Archer walked out from the back with a pot of coffee and two cups.

"I reckon you boys are hungry?" he asked as he set the pot and cups down on a table.

"As a bear coming out from a long winter," said Carmichael.

"Pearl is in the back cooking up some more grub," said Archer.

Carmichael's ears immediately perked up. "Pearl is here?" he asked.

"Yeah, for some reason, she came in and volunteered to cook for me this morning," he said as he filled both cups. "Good thing too 'cause I usually overcook everything."

They sat down and Carmichael kept shooting glances over at the door going back to the kitchen. Pearl finally came out carrying two large platters of food. She headed straight for their table and set the platters down in front of them.

"Good morning to you two," she said happily. "I hope this will satisfy your appetites."

Jess looked at the food and Carmichael kept staring at Pearl.

"It looks wonderful," said Jess as he picked up a fork from the plate. Carmichael just kept looking at Pearl and she leaned down and kissed him on the cheek.

"It's going to get cold if you don't start eating," she told him. He picked up his fork.

"Thank you, Pearl. It looks delicious," he told her. Jess smiled up at her and tapped his cheek.

She gave him a shrewd smile. "No kisses for you this time," she told Jess before spinning on her heels and scooting back into the kitchen.

"But that's not fair," Jess called to her.

She didn't turn. She just waved her hand in the air as she disappeared into the back. Carmichael was grinning widely again as he forked a chunk of ham and shoved it into his mouth.

Jess started cutting his ham and frowned. "Looks like someone has a favorite," he said.

Carmichael swallowed his ham and looked back at the kitchen. "I sure hope so," he said.

They finished eating and Jess left money on the table, along with twenty dollars on the bar for Archer. They retrieved their things from their rooms and headed for the livery. The young worker there had brushed their horses down and fed them a few apples. When they walked in,

Sharps snorted loudly and stomped his front right hoof as if he was anxious to get moving again.

"They sure do like apples," said the worker.

"Yes they do," acknowledged Jess.

"Are you two really going after the others who left?" the livery boy asked.

"Yep," replied Jess.

"Make sure you kill them when you catch up to them. That was my ma and pa they shot down in the middle of the street."

Jess put his hand on the worker's shoulder. "You can be sure of two things," he told him frankly. "One, we will catch every last one of them and two, when we do, they won't be breathing air when we finish with them." The worker nodded and walked into the back, his head hung low in sorrow.

They finished saddling their horses and walked them to the general store. No one was inside, so they took what they needed and left money on the counter for it. They walked out and climbed up in the saddle as Pearl stepped out of the saloon, shading her eyes from the morning sun. They turned their horses toward her and walked them over.

"You two take care of yourselves. Make sure you both come back," she told them.

"We will, after we finish what we started," Jess told her.

"And don't forget what I asked you," she said, looking straight at Jess.

"I won't," he said as they turned their horses toward the west end of town. Carmichael waved at her and she blew him a kiss.

They followed the wagon ruts until they found the large opening where the townsfolk had turned the wagon around. Jess got down off his horse and walked around. He found the four sets of horse tracks heading farther west along the trail. He walked along the trail until he saw a drop of dried blood on the rocky ground. He turned and headed back to where Carmichael waited.

"They went on horseback that way and one of them is leaving a trail of blood," he said. "Must be the one I shot after we blew up the privy back in town."

"Do you still think it's the Roper brothers?" asked Carmichael.

"I know it is," he said as he climbed up in the saddle. "Archer back at the saloon told me it was Lester and Elam Roper who left with the other two men."

"This trail leads to a town called Grover," said Carmichael.

"I'm betting they're heading there for a doctor."

"Ain't no doctor gonna keep them alive for long."

"We're in agreement on that," Jess said with a look of determination on his face as he nudged Gray into a slow gallop along the trail, looking down every so often at the dried drops of blood that seemed to get bigger and bigger.

CHAPTER TWENTY-EIGHT

Jess and Carmichael reached the town of Grover before dusk. They both could sense immediately that something bad had happened. They rode over to the jail, but it was locked up tight. They slid from the saddle and looked around. There were plenty of people out and milling about, talking to one another.

"Something happened here," said Carmichael.

"Yeah, and I bet the Ropers had something to do with it," said Jess as he looked over at the saloon. A few men were standing on the boardwalk talking to one another.

"Let's head to the saloon," said Jess. "Best place to get information if the jail is closed."

The two of them walked across to the saloon, aware of the multiple sets of eyes watching. The men standing outside cleared a path for them. Jess went in first after removing his hammer strap, followed by Carmichael, who did the same. The men outside whispered to one another and Carmichael heard Jess's name mentioned. The barkeep stood behind the bar talking to a few men. He noticed Jess immediately and moved away from the other men.

"Mr. Williams, I'm not surprised that you'd show up here now after what happened yesterday," he said as he reached behind him and grabbed a bottle of good whiskey and two glasses. "I didn't know you worked with a partner though."

"It's only temporary. What happened yesterday?"

"There was a slaughter over at the doctor's office," he said. "Some men murdered the doctor, town marshal and a prisoner who was a patient. There were four of them by the looks of the tracks we found leaving the back of the doctor's office."

"I bet I know who it was too," Jess told him.

"Who? No one in town saw who it was."

"Elam and Lester Roper and two of their thugs," Jess told him. "We trailed them here from Hades."

"You were in Hades?" asked the barkeep. "Did you see any demons or witches?"

"There never were any demons or witches in that town, only a gang of ruthless killers led by the Roper brothers and a bunch of innocent townsfolk."

"So you're going after them?"

"Yes, we are."

"Good, the marshal didn't have any deputies and we didn't know what to do," said the barkeep. "Some of the men in town talked about forming a posse, but it never seemed to happen. I guess no one wanted to be in charge of it."

"Better you leave them to us anyway," Jess told him as he took a sip of his whiskey just as a crack of thunder rolled through the town. Jess walked out to the batwings and saw the dark looming clouds way off in the distance.

He turned to Carmichael. "Finish that whiskey," he told him. "We've got to get a lead on their trail before that storm hits and washes away any tracks." Carmichael nodded, downed the whiskey and threw a silver dollar on the bar. He headed out of the saloon following Jess across the street to their horses.

They climbed up in the saddle and rode over to behind the doctor's office and examined the same four sets of shoe prints left by the horses they had trailed there. The tracks headed straight west and they followed them for a few miles before Jess halted his horses and pointed to some trees off the trail.

"We'd best get into those trees and set up camp before the rain hits," he said above the rumbling thunder and flashes of lightning that lit up the darkening sky.

Carmichael nodded and they headed for the trees. Jess took care of the horses while Carmichael gathered as much dry wood as he could find. After that, they worked quickly to put up a lean-to to get some cover from the rain that was just beginning to fall slowly. They got some things out of their saddlebags and untied their bedrolls before the rain started falling harder, the black, ominous-looking clouds reaching them.

They hadn't been under the tarp five minutes when the rain started pouring down in buckets. They even had to dig some furrows in the dirt to carry the rainwater away from their camp. After starting a fire, heating up some food and coffee, they both leaned against their saddles sipping coffee. Jess put a few more pieces of wood on the fire and poured himself another cup of coffee. He leaned back and looked at Carmichael, who had that faraway look in his eyes again.

"Back at the battlefront again?" Jess asked him.

Carmichael broke his gaze and shook his head. "No, I was just wondering if I could have any kind of normal life one day," he said dubiously. "After the war ended, I wandered around a lot, never going anywhere, never leaving anywhere. I started hiring my gun out for a while, but I eventually tired of that. It seems the only thing I'm built for is killing. That war really messed up a lot of men. Killing their own brothers because they were fighting on the other side. Things like that. Watching your friends dropping on the battlefield all around you. Yet I'm still alive to tell you about it.

"I remember one time when the fighting was as fierce as I've ever seen it. Men were dying all around me and I just stopped firing and stood there, waiting to catch a bullet, wanting it all to end, but it never happened. I must've stood there for a full five minutes before loading my rifle again and charging forward. I always wondered why I didn't die that day. Part of me wanted to, but it didn't happen. After that, they picked me to be a sniper. At first, I liked being alone most of the time. Hiding in a tree or a ditch waiting to pick off a soldier who never even knew I was there. After a while, it got harder to pull the trigger. Truth be told, I let a few dozen men live, not that they'd ever know it."

Jess looked at him seriously. "You're a good man on the inside, Jason Carmichael. You did what you were ordered to do and you can't fault yourself for that. As for having a normal life, you've got a pretty woman back in Hades, or whatever they're renaming it. You might have a chance to start a new life with her if you play your cards right. I'm certain that she's sweet on you."

Carmichael chuckled and shook his head. "Yeah, and now, after all the battles I've fought, after standing in that field with bullets whizzing past me for five minutes, I'll probably get shot dead or fall off my horse and break my neck."

"Or you could challenge me after we finish with the Ropers and their men," chuckled Jess. "That would get you killed for sure."

"Anyone ever tell you that you're a little bit cocky?"

"More than once, but I call it confidence."

"Well, we ain't gonna find out because I've decided against that," he said smiling. "I knew my brother was troubled and riding with the wrong people. It was only a matter of time before he got himself killed or locked up behind bars. I can't blame you for it now that I've had some time to think on it."

"I'm glad to hear that because I really didn't want to put a bullet in you."

"See, there's that cockiness again," laughed Carmichael.

"Well, let's get some shut-eye and see what we can find tomorrow," said Jess. "Tracks will be washed out, but they seem to be headed straight west. The town of Stony Creek is in that direction and I bet they have a doctor in town."

"Sounds good to me," agreed Carmichael. They crawled into their bedrolls, both with their pistols on their laps. A few minutes passed by and Carmichael lifted his head.

"You absolutely certain you're faster than me?"

"Absolutely," replied Jess without even opening his eyes.

* * *

The four men sat atop their saddles outside the town of Stony Creek. Elam's head was slumped down on his chest.

Rivard and Lester sat next to him to keep him from falling out of the saddle. Elam had finished the first bottle of laudanum and was working on the second one, but he was so out of it now, he was barely conscious.

"How much longer are we gonna wait?" asked Rivard.

"Until a few more of the lamps go out," said Lester. "We want to sneak in and get out without the town law catching us."

Dorathy, who sat on his horse in front of them, turned his head around. "I checked the doctor's office earlier and it's a house and office combined," he advised. "His office is in the back, so we can break in there, force him to tend to Elam and get out. Since they live there, we can take all the food they have so we don't have to break into the general store. I saw a woman inside too. I figure it must be his wife."

"Good, the less time we spend there the better," said Lester as he reached out and pushed Elam back up against his horse's neck.

"How much of that stuff did he drink?" Rivard asked.

"He's a quarter of the way through the second bottle, but I took it away from him when he was passed out earlier," said Lester. "I think he's already hooked on the stuff."

"Well, at least it doesn't look like he's feeling any pain," said Rivard.

"I don't think he's feeling anything at all," Lester frowned as he kept hold of Elam. A little while later, Dorathy turned in the saddle after checking his watch.

"I think it's safe to go in now," he told Lester, who nodded and kept his hand on Elam's arm as they started moving forward.

They stayed in the shadows as much as they could. They walked their horses around the town and then rode straight up to the back of the doctor's office and house. Before dismounting, they looked around at the surrounding buildings, but most were already dark. Only a few of them had oil lamps turned down low.

Lester glanced over at Rivard. "You and Dorathy go in and secure the doc and his wife and then one of you come back and help me get him inside," whispered Lester.

Rivard and Dorathy slid from their saddles and walked to the back door. Rivard tried the door handle and smiled when he found it unlocked. He slowly opened it and walked in, pulling his pistol out as he did. Dorathy followed behind him. They went through the doctor's office first, which consisted of a long hallway and three rooms, each with a metal table and medicinal items. They got to the end of the hallway and entered the living room, which was spacious with plenty of furniture around. An oil lamp burned on a small table by the front door.

Rivard tapped Dorathy on his shoulder and pointed to the stairway going up to the second floor. They carefully made their way upstairs. There were three doors along the upstairs hallway, but only one of them was partially open, with a dim light coming from inside the room.

Rivard slowly pushed the door open with the barrel of his pistol and saw a middle-aged woman sleeping in a large bed. He quietly walked heel to toe toward her until he was able to place the gun barrel against her cheek. She slowly opened her eyes as she heard the metallic clicking sounds the pistol made when he thumbed the hammer back.

"Who are you, and what do you want?" she asked.

"We have someone who needs a doctor."

"My husband isn't home yet."

"Then get dressed and let's go downstairs and wait for him," he told her as he backed up enough for her to get out of bed. She put her spectacles on and reached for a heavy robe that was on the bedpost. She stood up and looked at both men, squinting her eyes to focus.

"Who the hell are you two?" she asked.

"You can't see our faces?" asked Rivard.

"Not much. Your faces are all blurry," she said. "Damn spectacles are useless anymore."

"That might be the best thing that has happened to you today," Rivard told her as he removed the spectacles and threw them onto the bed. "Let's go downstairs and wait for your husband."

Once Dorathy had the woman sitting in a chair while he guarded the front door, Rivard went outside to help Lester bring Elam in through the back door. Elam could walk, but only with support. Lester and Rivard put him on one of the tables in a room off the hallway. Lester stayed with Elam and Rivard went back into the living room. He turned to the woman as he pulled out his long-bladed knife.

"Do you know what this is?" he asked her.

She strained to focus on it. "Some kind of stick?"

"No, it's a very sharp knife and if you try to call out or warn your husband, I'll cut your throat wide open with it," he warned her. She folded her hands together and sat still.

Rivard turned to Dorathy. "Go to the kitchen and get what food we can use and pack our saddlebags with it," he told him. "As soon as Elam is tended to, we'll leave."

Dorathy headed for the kitchen and started riffling through the cupboards. Rivard stood by the front door with his pistol in his hand while watching the woman and waiting for the doctor to come home.

* * *

Doctor Deke Compton threw his cards down on the table with a disgruntled look on his face. He had lost almost every hand to the other three men at the table.

"Well, boys, I'm about all cleaned out," he said frowning.

"Aw, come on, Doc. You can still play a few more hands," cackled one of the men. Compton took out his gold pocket watch and looked at the time.

"The missus is going to give me hell already for being out this late," he frowned as he finished the last of his whiskey. "I'm afraid you boys will have to continue without me."

Compton stood up and walked out of the saloon. He headed along the boardwalk toward his house and office. He crossed over two streets and saw the dim light in the window. He opened the wooden gate to his front yard and walked to the front door. When he opened it, he saw a man standing behind his wife, holding a knife to her throat.

"Welcome home, Doc," said Rivard. "Now, close the door and don't try anything stupid."

"That's right," scowled Dorathy as he walked out of the kitchen with a mouthful of cake and pointed a pistol at Compton.

CHAPTER TWENTY-NINE

In the morning, the rain had stopped, but there was a heavy mist in the air making the first rays of sunlight a dreary gray color. After heating some food and coffee, the two of them proceeded to take down the lean-to and hang their bedrolls on branches to dry. When they were dry, they saddled up and headed out. The tracks left by the Ropers were completely washed away.

Jess and Carmichael rode into the town of Stony Creek a few hours later. The sun was still shining brightly and not too many people were out. They rode straight down the main street and saw the jail. They started heading for it when Jess put his hand up as he halted his horses.

"What is it?" asked Carmichael, sliding his rifle out after seeing the look on Jess's face.

"Look over at the bank," he told him as he slid his Winchester out.

Carmichael looked at the bank and immediately noticed what Jess was looking at. There were four horses in front of the bank and two of them had men sitting in the saddle, each with a rifle across his lap. Both of them were constantly glancing around the town.

"That doesn't look right," said Carmichael.

Jess noticed the door to the jail opening and a man with a shiny star pinned to his shirt came walking out. He was looking directly at Jess and Carmichael and holding a sawed-off in his hands. He started to head toward them when Jess pointed to the two men sitting atop their horses in front of the bank. The marshal glanced over his shoulder toward the bank just as one of the men raised his rifle and fired at him. The slug smacked into the marshal's back and he stumbled forward a few steps before falling into the dusty street. Jess and Carmichael aimed at the two men.

"Take the closest one," said Jess as he fired his rifle one second before Carmichael did.

The two men flew sideways off their horses as two more men came running out of the bank. Each had a bank bag in one hand and a pistol in the other. One of them fired two shots into the bank while the other one fired a shot at Jess and Carmichael, missing Carmichael's head by a foot. Jess levered another round in and fired.

The man who fired at Carmichael went down. The other turned around and jumped on his horse. He fired a shot back toward Jess and Carmichael, but Carmichael fired again and the slug hit the man in the back, throwing him against his horse's neck. The horse kept running as the man slowly slid from the saddle.

By now, a dozen men were out in the street brandishing shotguns and rifles, but it was over. Two men were turning the marshal over to check on him. He was bleeding badly. Jess and Carmichael slid from the saddle and walked over to the marshal.

He looked up at Jess with a pained expression. "I'm glad you showed up when you did," he said. "I'm Marshal Tad Hack."

"Nice to meet you, Marshal, but you'd better send someone out to fetch that other horse that has the other bank bag of money on the saddle," Jess told him.

The marshal pointed to one man without saying a word and the man ran to the nearest horse he could fine. He jumped in the saddle and heeled the horse out of town. Carmichael watched as two men from the bank walked out and made sure the three men were dead. They carried the bank bag back inside. The man who fetched the other horse came riding back in with the bank bag still wrapped around the saddle horn. One of the men kneeling down by the marshal looked down the street.

"Where in the hell is Doc Compton?" he asked. Jess glanced warily at Carmichael, who nodded perceptively.

"You'd better take us to the doctor's house," Jess told the man. The marshal waved at the man to do so and he stood up.

"Follow me," he said as he started walking. "Do you two know something we don't know?"

"I sure hope not," Jess told him. "But we've been tracking four killers and we think they came here to get some medical attention for one of them I shot."

The man led them to the two-story house with a white picket fence and flowers planted all around it. The man opened the gate, went to the front door and rapped hard on it. There was no answer. He rapped on it again, harder.

"Doc, are you in there?" he shouted. "The marshal's been shot and he needs you."

Jess moved the man aside, leaned his rifle against the front wall and pulled his pistol out. He turned the handle and pushed the door open slowly to reveal a woman in a heavy robe tied to a chair. She had a towel stuffed in her mouth held by a piece of rope. Her eyes went wide with fear and she shook her head violently.

"Anyone else in here?" he asked. She nodded affirmatively. Carmichael walked in holding his pistol with his thumb on the hammer and Jess motioned for him to check the rest of the lower level, keeping his attention on the upstairs. He glanced at the man who'd brought them there.

"Untie her from that chair," Jess told him as he kept watching the upstairs. The man did and she let out a huge gasp when he pulled the towel from her mouth.

"Miltz, where's the doc?" the man asked her as Carmichael walked in from the back office area.

"He's dead," he said. "Someone cut him wide open, but he had to have been working on someone back there. There's lots of bandages and bloody tools in the room where the doctor is. Sorry, ma'am." The woman ran toward the back and a few seconds later, she let out a blood-curdling scream.

"It had to be the Ropers and their men," Jess told Carmichael.

"The Roper brothers?" asked the man. "I thought they was in Hades."

"They were until we chased them out and trailed them here," Jess told him as they saw some men carrying the marshal toward the house.

They walked inside and took him into one of the empty rooms and gently placed him on the table. The woman was sobbing now as she held her husband's head in her lap. One of the men walked to the doorway and stood there. He removed his hat and held it against his chest.

"Miltz, I'm really sorry about the doc, but the marshal is bleeding pretty badly," he said apologetically. She looked up at him with tears flowing down her cheeks.

"Just give me a few minutes," she sobbed. "Cut his shirt off for me." He nodded, put his hat back on and headed into the room with the marshal. Jess and Carmichael holstered their pistols and stayed in the front room as more men sauntered in.

Carmichael gave Jess a cautious look. "Should I check the upstairs," he asked Jess.

"I don't think so. Let's go out back and check for tracks," Jess told him.

The two of them walked along the hallway until they reached the back door. They opened it and immediately saw all the footprints and horse tracks riding in and leaving. Jess walked out a ways and noticed the blood drops in the sand coming toward the house. He walked back to Carmichael.

"The one who's wounded was bleeding when he arrived and not when he left."

"Looks like they're still headed west," said Carmichael.

"Yeah, and by the looks of their tracks, they ain't moving real fast, so we should be able to catch up with them soon," said Jess.

"Should we leave now?"

"No, let's wait and see if we can talk to the marshal first. Maybe he can give us some information."

"Let's go get our horses and get a bite to eat while they work on him," suggested Carmichael.

Jess nodded and they walked around the house to their horses. Carmichael checked his saddlebags for the money inside. After they ate at a local café, they walked their horses down to the doctor's house and went inside. Several men were standing around.

"How's the marshal?" Jess asked one of them.

"Miltz is finishing up with him right now," he said. "Looks like he's gonna be okay."

Jess and Carmichael walked along the hallway until they came to the room where the marshal was. Miltz was washing blood off her hands and the marshal was propped up and awake. He saw Jess and smiled slightly.

"If you hadn't shown up, I might not be here hurting like hell," said the marshal. "What brought you to my town anyway?"

"We've been hunting the Roper brothers and two other men. I'm certain they're the ones who did this," replied Jess.

"Damn Roper brothers," coughed the marshal. "They're as cold-blooded as they come. I just received new wanted posters in my office on them. They raised the bounty to ten thousand on each of their heads. I hope you catch those bastards."

"We will, but we don't know much about the other two men who are with them. We've actually never got a clear look at either of the brothers."

"I might be able to help with that," said Miltz as she turned around at the sink and pulled her spectacles off.

"How?" asked Jess.

"I only need these things to see close up," she said. "I saw the other two men clearly."

Marshal Hack looked over at one of the other men in the room. "Go to the jail, get my stack of wanted posters from my desk and take the ones on the Roper brothers off the wall and bring them here," he told him. The man ran out and over to the jail.

"So, you could identify the other two men who tied you up?" Jess asked Miltz.

"Of course," she said. "I let them think I was blind without my spectacles, which is probably the only reason I'm still alive. I can even draw a likeness if you want."

"That would be really helpful if you could do that," said Jess.

"I'll get on it right away," she said as she walked out and headed for the kitchen where she had paper and a pencil.

Carmichael turned to Jess. "I hope those other two have bounties on their heads too," he said.

"Me too, but we're killing them anyway," said Jess as he turned back to the marshal.

"Marshal, if we bring you the Ropers and the other two men back here, can the town pay the bounty on all four of them?" he asked.

"After what you did today, foiling that bank robbery and probably saving my life, yes," he said most assuredly as the man came running back with the wanted posters.

He handed the two on the Roper brothers to Jess to look at. Elam and Lester were both wanted dead or alive for ten thousand each. The marshal flipped through the stack of other wanted posters until he found one on Saul Rivard and one on Ben Dorathy. He handed them to Jess.

Both of these men have been known to ride with the Ropers," said the marshal.

Jess looked at both wanted posters. Rivard was worth two thousand and Dorathy was worth three. Both were wanted dead or alive for a long list of heinous crimes. Jess was looking at the ones on Rivard and Dorathy when Miltz came scooting in with two pencil sketches that matched their wanted posters. She handed them to Jess and he compared them and smiled.

"You sure can draw," he told her.

"I was always going to be an artist, but when I married my husband, I worked as his assistant and just never got to painting or drawing much after that," she said as she started sniffling. "You make sure those men pay for what they've done."

"We will, I promise," he told her as he turned to the marshal.

"Marshal, we found their tracks out behind the house. I don't think they can move that fast with one of them badly wounded," Jess told him. "I reckon we'll be back in a few days hauling four dead bodies."

"It couldn't be soon enough," grimaced the marshal. "Doctor Compton was a well-respected man in this town."

"One more thing, Marshal," said Jess. "Have you heard of any bank robberies in the last month or so where thirty thousand dollars was taken?"

"No, I'd know about any bank robberies," he said. "Especially if it's one that happened close by because we'd be watching to see if we got hit next. That's why we were so surprised by what happened today." Jess shook the marshal's hand and he and Carmichael walked out to their horses.

Carmichael looked at Jess. "So, if the money I took off those two men wasn't from a bank robbery, where did it come from?"

"No way of telling for sure," said Jess. "They could have taken it off some rancher or anyone who had some money hidden."

"Then why were they talking about robbing a bank?"

"They might have just been bragging and telling a tale."

They retrieved their horses and started following the tracks for a few miles until Jess stopped his horses.

Carmichael reined in his horse and turned in the saddle. "What is it?"

Jess leaned over and saw the drop of dried blood in the sand. "Looks like the wounded one is already bleeding again," he said as he straightened in the saddle and took his spyglass out to scan the landscape up ahead.

"Good," said Carmichael. "That'll slow them down."

"I'm bettin' that doctor back there left the stitches loose, knowing they'll come loose and he'd start bleeding again."

CHAPTER THIRTY

Elam fell off his horse for the third time in the last hour. He landed face down and passed out cold. Lester and Rivard jumped out of the saddle and rolled him over. His wound was bleeding badly and the blood was soaking through the bandage material.

"Damn stitches must've came loose," carped Lester.

"Maybe that doctor did that on purpose," said Rivard.

Elam opened his eyes and looked at the sky. "Am I dead?" he asked.

"No, but your wound is bleeding again," said Lester.

"Give me some more laudanum."

"You don't need any more of that shit," spat Lester.

"But it hurts."

"It's supposed to," said Lester. "Can you ride your horse?"

"I'm not on him now?"

"No, you idiot," growled Lester as he looked at Rivard. "We're gonna have to find a spot to hole up and let him rest." Rivard nodded as he started helping Lester lift Elam off the ground and get him back on his horse.

"Hang onto the saddle horn until we find a place to make camp where we're out of sight," blustered Lester with frustration plastered on his face.

They started their horses again and rode for another few hours before Dorathy pointed to a heavily wooded area up ahead off the trail. Lester nodded and they headed straight for it. A while later, they carefully rode into the woods and found a small clearing that someone had obviously used as a camp before.

There was an old fire pit dug out of the ground and lined with rocks. A small stream ran close by and Dorathy busied himself with tethering the horses on a long rope near it that allowed them access to the stream and plenty of grass to graze on. Lester and Rivard got Elam onto his bedroll and then started collecting wood to start a fire. After they ate a meal, Lester took the plate from Elam, who looked up at him pleadingly.

"Brother, I need another sip of that stuff."

"But it's messing your head up," Lester argued.

"I know, I know, but just one more sip to relieve the pain," Elam begged. Lester put the plate down and handed Elam the bottle. He took it, uncorked it and started drinking it as fast as he could.

"Give me that," growled Lester angrily as he wrestled the bottle away from him. He poured the rest of the laudanum out on the ground and threw the bottle away in the woods.

"What the hell did you do that for?" wailed Elam.

"Because if you keep drinking that stuff you'll never get back to normal," argued Lester.

"I'm still the leader of this outfit."

"Not until you get your wits about you. You haven't made a decision since you started drinking that stuff."

Elam started reaching for his pistol and found it wasn't in his holster. "Hey, where did my gun go?"

"I took that off you back at the last doctor's office," said Lester.

"What doctor?"

"See what I mean?" explained Lester as he waved his hands around in the air. "We stopped in another town and got your wound cleaned and patched and you don't even remember it."

"I was probably sleeping."

"You were mostly passed out from that laudanum."

"Well, I want my gun back."

"No, not until you can be trusted not to shoot one of us for not giving you any more of that stuff. It's gone anyway now, so you ain't gettin' any more."

"You shouldn't have done that," said Elam.

"You can eat some beans and then sleep through the night," said Lester. "Maybe tomorrow we can get back on the trail again."

Elam started to say something, but Rivard handed him a tin plate of beans and salt pork and he started eating it. Rivard rolled his eyes at Lester and he nodded as if he knew. Dorathy just sat there watching Elam eating his food, wondering to himself if he shouldn't just sneak out of camp during his turn at watch and get away from them.

* * *

Jess and Carmichael rode pretty hard, following the tracks and drops of dried blood. When Jess saw the tracks veering off the trail heading west, he skidded his horses to a quick halt. Carmichael rode another twenty feet or so before stopping and turning in the saddle. He turned his horse around as Jess leaned over to examine the tracks.

"What?" asked Carmichael.

"They changed directions," said Jess as he kept looking at the ground.

Carmichael saw the tracks where they turned off. "They sure did," he agreed as he turned in the saddle to look in the direction the tracks went.

"Don't look that way," Jess said quickly.

"Why not?"

"There's a wooded area way off in that direction and if they went inside there, they could be watching us through some field glasses. I don't want them to think we found where they turned off."

"Okay, so what do you want to do?"

"Act as if we didn't notice it and continue riding straight west past the woods."

"But what if they're not in there and just rode through them to cover their tracks?"

"I've been counting the drops of blood along the way and whoever is wounded has lost a lot of it. Maybe enough that he can't sit in a saddle upright."

"So, you want to keep riding west and come back through the woods at the other end?"

"Exactly," said Jess as he climbed up in the saddle, reached into his back pocket and pulled out some beef jerky. He tore it in half and handed the other piece to Carmichael.

"This is lunch?"

"Yeah, if they're watching, they might think we just stopped for a bite and took a minute to rest our horses."

"You've learned a lot of tricks about hunting men," acknowledged Carmichael as he chewed on the jerky.

"It's all I do, so after a while you learn to think like the hunted," said Jess.

"Ever thought about taking a break?"

"Yeah, a few times, but I just seem to keep at it."

"I guess I know the feeling. But I think I'm finally ready for a change in my life."

"Would that have anything to do with a pretty woman back in Hades by the name of Pearl?"

"She sure is pretty and I think she's someone who can handle me," said Carmichael.

"That's a lot of handling," mused Jess.

"You didn't have to agree so easily."

Jess took a sip from a canteen and handed it to Carmichael. When he finished, he handed it back to Jess. They turned their horses due west and put them into a moderate gallop, making sure neither of them looked over in the direction of the woods.

Back in the trees, standing behind a large oak, Dorathy kept watching them through his large field glasses. When he saw them riding west again, he smiled and turned to Rivard and Lester, who stood behind him with their rifles in their hands.

"That bounty hunter ain't so smart after all," he cackled. "They're heading west again."

"You don't think they saw where we turned off?" asked Lester.

"Naw, they stopped and ate some jerky or something in the saddle, but they never even looked this way," said Dorathy. "They knew we were heading west all along. When the rain washed our tracks out before, they still followed us west, so they still think that's the way we're heading."

"Good," said Lester. "Tomorrow, we head south through the woods and lose them for good."

"I agree," said Rivard. Dorathy watched them until they were completely out of sight before returning to the camp, where Elam was snoring loudly.

CHAPTER THIRTY-ONE

Jess and Carmichael rode about six miles farther west before turning toward the wooded area. When they reached it, they rode inside a good hundred yards before heading to where they figured the Ropers might be camped. The brush was thick and the branches were low. They found themselves ducking and moving branches out of their way. When they found a good spot a safe distance from where they estimated the camp might be, they stopped for the night and made a small fire to heat up some coffee. They ate cold beans and peaches.

"When we get back to Hades, I'm going to eat the biggest meal I can get," said Carmichael as he threw his empty can of peaches away. He poured himself another cup of coffee and started to put a few more twigs onto the smoldering fire.

"Don't put any more wood on that fire," Jess told him.

"All right," he said. "I'll take first watch while you get some sleep."

"Okay, but wake me if you see any evidence of a fire," he agreed as he leaned against a large tree.

"You're still assuming they're in these woods?"

"I'm betting on it," he said as he slid his hat over his eyes.

Carmichael let the tiny fire die down to a few glowing embers, just enough to keep the coffee warm enough to drink. He sat on a dead tree log with his rifle in his hands, looking eastward through the thick trees. His eyelids started slowly closing. He quickly caught himself and shook the sleepiness from his head. He looked eastward again and thought he caught a glimpse of orange. He picked up a twig and threw it at Jess. He woke quickly, throwing the blanket off him.

"See something?"

"I'm not sure, but I could swear I caught a sign of a fire straight that way," he said pointing. Jess got his spyglass out of his saddlebags and peered through it. After a few moments, he saw an orange flash just bright enough for him to see it.

"You're right," said Jess. "Someone is camped out there about two miles from us."

"It could be hunters," he said. "Men being hunted wouldn't usually keep a fire going this late at night."

"Unless they thought we were long gone."

"You might be right since we rode a good distance from where they turned off before riding back in here." Jess put the spyglass down on the log and pulled out his pocket watch to check the time.

"It'll be light in a few hours," he said as he stuffed the watch back in his pocket. "I say we take our rifles, both of my buffalo guns and make our way slowly through the trees on foot. We can be ready for them when they wake in the morning. We need to make sure it ain't some hunters before we open fire though."

"Okay," said Carmichael. "Let's get ready. I hope it's them though, 'cause I want to finish this and get back to Hades."

"I'll bet you do."

Jess took the spyglass and the pouch of custom-loaded cartridges with him, along with one of his buffalo rifles, a Winchester, a canteen and some jerky. Carmichael took his rifle and Jess's other buffalo rifle. The two of them started slowly walking toward the camp. Both of them avoided stepping on branches or making any noises that might alert whoever was in the camp.

When they were about seven hundred yards away, they both became slower and much more cautious, trying to always have a tree between themselves and the camp. When they were three hundred yards away, they stopped. Jess handed Carmichael a handful of the custom-loaded cartridges. He stuffed them into his front pockets.

"I assume you have extra rounds for your rifle?" Jess whispered quietly.

"Are you really asking me that?" he whispered as he felt the bulge of rifle shells in his other pocket. "I never go into battle without plenty of ammunition."

"Listen, if it's the Ropers and their men, we give them one warning and then we cut them down like the dogs they are."

"I didn't plan on taking any prisoners," agreed Carmichael.

"Remember, shoot at anyone on the right and I'll shoot anyone on the left so we don't waste shots," he reminded Carmichael, who simply nodded.

"Move about twenty feet that way so they have to shoot at two targets," Jess told him.

"Got it," he whispered. "Stay low and don't get killed, soldier. This might be my last battle and I want both of us to be the ones walking away."

Carmichael moved away until he found a nice spot between two smaller trees where he could fire from safely. He took his hat off and propped the barrel of the rifle on top of it. He quietly chambered a round in and waited. Jess nestled himself by a large oak tree. He found a rock large enough to prop his rifle barrel on and chambered a round into it. He took his hat off and set it behind the tree.

A few hours later, the first rays of sunlight started filtering into the woods. The air was crisp and chilly with morning dew lingering in the air. Rivard was on guard duty, but his eyes were closed as he leaned against a dead tree close to the fire. He woke and yawned. He slowly stood up and put several pieces of wood on the fire, rubbing his hands together as the flames quickly came to life.

Lester stirred and opened his eyes as he lay there. Jess threw a twig at Carmichael, who was watching intently, his sights already on the back of Rivard, although he didn't know who it was. Jess extended the spyglass and looked at the man standing. When he turned around, he saw it was Saul Rivard. He looked over at Carmichael and put his hand up, telling him to wait until he could make sure the Ropers were there.

Lester rubbed his eyes and looked over at Elam, who was still passed out from the laudanum and loss of blood. He slowly threw his blanket off and sat straight up, looking at the fire. He saw the coffee pot sitting on a rock by the fire.

"Any coffee left?" he asked.

Rivard shook his head. "Naw, I drank the last of it earlier," he said. "I'll make another pot." Lester shook Elam, but he just moaned in his sleep.

"We're gonna have to get him to another doctor," said Lester.

"I'm not sure he's gonna make it much farther," cautioned Rivard.

"We shouldn't have given him that laudanum," said Lester.

"Maybe, but I still think that last doctor screwed up those stitches on purpose so he'd bleed out slowly."

"We should go back there and kill his wife," said Lester as he slowly stood up and stretched.

Jess saw him through the spyglass. He closed it and looked over at Carmichael, who was waiting for the sign. Jess nodded and raised his thumb in the air, letting him know to go ahead. Lester was on the left, so Jess took careful aim and slowly started squeezing back on the trigger until the rifle roared in the silence of the morning.

The three hundred seventy-five grain slug hurled through the air and punched a hole straight through Lester's right side, spinning him sideways. Blood spurted out of his backside as he stumbled and fell over a dead log.

Carmichael fired a split second later, the slug almost tearing Rivard's left arm off at the elbow as he turned to see where the firing had come from. He screamed and pulled his pistol out, firing in that direction. Jess and Carmichael knew they were out of range from any pistol fire and even out of range from any rifle fire, except in the hands of an expert marksman. Dorathy jumped out of his bedroll, his rifle in his hands. He crawled to the dead tree Lester was

221

behind, wailing from the pain. He rolled over it and looked at Lester's two bloody hands.

"How bad are you hit?" he asked.

Lester looked at his side where the blood was pushing out with each heartbeat. "I'm hit bad," he wailed. "It's gotta be that damn bounty hunter."

"But they rode by us until they were out of sight," said Dorathy as he rose up and fired two shots from his rifle. Rivard was lying behind a log looking at his elbow, which was dangling by the meat on each side. His elbow was shattered into pieces.

"Son of a bitch!" he cursed as he raised his pistol and emptied it in the direction the shots were coming from. Just as he ducked back down, a slug tore off a large chunk of bark right where his head had been a second earlier. Elam woke up and lifted his head. His eyes were bleary and unfocused and his brain was foggy from the lingering effects of the laudanum still working on him.

"What the hell is happening?" he called out, too weak to even sit up.

"Stay down, Elam," yelled Lester as another slug slammed into the log he was sitting behind, still holding his side, the blood pumping through his fingers.

Rivard was using one hand to reload his pistol. When he had it loaded, he turned, rose up to fire, but everything went totally black as the heavy-caliber slug entered his right eye and blew part of his brains out the back of his skull. He fell behind the log, dead and motionless.

Dorathy levered another round into his rifle and called out. "You cowards," he shouted loudly. "Come on out and fight like men!"

Jess finished chambering another round into his rifle and placed the barrel on the rock. "You mean like the way you killed the doctor and marshal in Grover or the way you killed the doctor in Stony Creek?" hollered Jess as he aimed at the spot where he figured Dorathy was positioned behind the log.

"We had to do that so there were no witnesses," argued Dorathy.

"And all the innocent people you and your men slaughtered in Hades? Burning women alive on a cross, shooting them down in the street like their lives didn't matter?"

"That was just business," hollered Dorathy.

"Yeah, well this is just business, killing cold-blooded murderers like you. We ain't giving you any chance at getting away," hollered Jess as he kept his finger on the trigger, aiming at the spot, waiting for Dorathy to raise his head. "Ain't one of you leaving here alive. Your reign of terror ends right here and right now."

Lester's hand slowly slid from his side as death finally claimed his body. Dorathy watched it and cursed under his breath. He raised his head up, deciding to empty his rifle in the direction where Jess and Carmichael were. But before he could pull the trigger, two heavy-caliber slugs smacked into the top of his forehead, tearing part of his skull away.

His body flew backward, dead before he hit the dirt. Jess laid the rifle butt down on the ground and picked up his Winchester as he nodded at Carmichael, who was already doing the same. Jess put up three fingers and Carmichael knew what that meant.

The two of them levered rounds into their rifles. They slowly made their way toward the camp, darting from one tree to another. When they got close to the camp, they waited for a few minutes to see if they caught any movement or drew any fire. They saw nothing. Jess motioned for Carmichael to go around to the right as Jess kept his rifle aimed at the camp, ready to pick off anything that moved. Carmichael finally made it far enough to see Lester and Dorathy's dead bodies. He saw Rivard slumped face down in the dirt behind a log.

"I count three down for sure," he called out to Jess, who moved toward the camp until he saw Elam still in his bedroll, passed out.

"I got Elam covered, although I don't think he's much of a threat," said Jess.

Carmichael walked into the camp and up next to him. "Is he breathing?" he asked.

"Yeah, but he seems to be passed out, probably from the lack of blood."

"Or he drank too much laudanum, because I found an empty bottle on the ground as I made my way here." Jess walked closer and pushed the barrel of his rifle against Elam's chest. He moaned as he opened his blurry eyes.

"Brother, why the hell are you poking me with that?" Elam demanded.

"I ain't your brother. He's dead and so are your partners.

"No they're not," he argued as he slurred his words.

"Elam Roper, you're wanted dead or alive for a list of crimes so long I won't bother to read them to you," Jess told him as he moved the barrel of his rifle up to his forehead. "I'm only sorry you don't really know who's sending you to hell, but maybe the devil will tell you when you get there."

"Huh?" stammered Elam with his eyes crossed as he starred at the rifle barrel. Elam had a split second of realization before Jess pulled the trigger.

"Bounty hunter?" he mumbled.

"That's right," said Jess as he pulled the trigger. The slug traveled through Elam's foggy brain and lodged into the dirt underneath him. His lifeless eyes stared up at the sky.

Carmichael sat down on the log by the fire. "Damn, all four down and neither of us got shot again," he said as he looked at Elam in his bedroll.

Jess leaned his rifle against the log and picked up the pot of coffee. "I'd say we deserve a hot cup of coffee," he told Carmichael.

"Why not?" agreed Carmichael. "I'm sure these boys won't object."

CHAPTER THIRTY-TWO

Jess and Carmichael took time to make breakfast with what they found in the men's saddlebags. After that, they tied the men across their saddles. They retrieved their horses and made their way out of the woods.

When they rode into Stony Creek, some of the townsfolk whistled and cheered. They trotted up to the jail where a man was sitting outside in a chair with a shotgun across his lap. He stood up and looked at the four dead bodies on the horses.

"Are those the four who killed Doctor Compton?" he asked.

"They are," said Jess as he and Carmichael slid from the saddle.

"The marshal is sitting at his desk," he said. "Give me the wanted posters on their sorry asses and I'll make an identification for the marshal. He can't move very good." Jess handed him the wanted posters. He walked to the bodies, identified all four and looked back over at them.

"You boys just made some real money," he said as he untied the horses. Jess and Carmichael walked inside and saw the marshal sitting behind his desk with his arm in a sling.

"Did you get every one of them sons of bitches?" Marshal Hack asked.

"All four of them," said Jess.

"I'll have my temporary deputy take the paperwork to the bank as soon as I have it filled out proper," he said smiling.

"Marshal, have you heard anything else about a bank robbery or anyone getting robbed of thirty thousand dollars?" queried Jess. He shook his head.

"No, nothing at all, but those men who tried to rob our bank would have gotten away with over fifty thousand dollars if you hadn't stopped them," he said.

"Thanks, Marshal," said Jess. "We're gonna get a hot meal while we wait for our money."

"Try Trudy's down the street," he suggested. "She's the best cook in town." They walked their horses to the café and ordered a huge meal. They were finishing their coffee when a man dressed in a very nice suit walked in and headed for their table.

"Mr. Williams, I want to personally thank you for foiling that bank robbery the other day," he said as he shook hands with Jess. "I have all your money right here. Twenty-five thousand. I wanted to deliver it to you myself." He handed Jess an envelope and Jess looked inside.

"Thanks for getting it so quickly," said Jess as the man was shaking hands with Carmichael.

"It was my pleasure," he said as he turned and left.

Carmichael looked at the envelope. "This bounty hunting business pays very well," he announced as he looked at the thick envelope.

Jess saw the look on his face and tilted his head slightly. "Don't even think about it," he told him. "You've got thirty thousand dollars in your saddlebags and you're getting half of this. That's enough money to last you a lifetime."

Carmichael leaned back in his chair and smiled. "So, you think that I should keep that money in my saddlebags?"

"Yeah, put it into a bank and wait to see if you hear about any robbery," he said. "After a while, consider it yours."

"I'm gonna build me the biggest house in Hades," he said.

Jess unbuttoned his shirt enough to stick the envelope inside and buttoned it back up again. "Speaking of Hades, let's get going," Jess told him as he put his hat on and stood up. They rode out of Stony Creek heading east toward Hades. They rode in silence for a few hours when Carmichael raised his hand and halted his horse.

"Did you see something?" asked Jess. Carmichael lowered his head for a moment and then pursed his lips.

"I gotta know," he said as he swiveled his head over to Jess.

"Know what?"

"If you're really faster than me."

"I am, so let's keep moving."

"How do you know for sure?"

"What does it matter now?"

"It matters to me."

"Why?"

"Because I was going to brace you when I first found you. Now, after all we've been through together, and with me maybe starting a new life, a better life, I need to know if I never would have made it to where I am right now. Sitting in this saddle. Having more money than I could ever have dreamed of. I need to know if it never would have happened."

Jess shook his head. "I don't want to kill you," he told Carmichael.

"And I don't want to kill you. But I still have to know. So, let's just draw side by side and see who's faster."

"I don't usually do that sort of thing."

"Come on, no one is here to see it but me and you and all we're gonna do is shoot a couple cans of beans."

Jess stared at him for a long minute. After seeing the serious look in his eyes, he finally relented. "Okay, but we're only doing this once and never again," he told Carmichael, who slid from the saddle and got two cans of beans out of his saddlebags.

He walked about twenty feet away and set the two cans on the ground about ten feet apart. Then, he heard the metallic clicks of a pistol being thumbed back and he slowly turned around. Jess stood there with his pistol in his hand, pointing it straight up in the air.

Carmichael let out a long breath and grinned. "That wasn't funny," he said.

"I was just checking my gun," Jess said, chuckling as he released the hammer and holstered his pistol.

Carmichael walked up and looked at it sitting in the holster. "Where did you get that thing anyway? I've never seen one like it before."

"I found it in my pa's barn one day."

"Ever seen one like it again?"

"No, but I look all the time."

"Okay, your can is on the left and I'll shoot at the one on the right," he said as he turned around and stood next to Jess, who put his hands into position.

"You gonna count or something?" Jess asked.

ROBERT J. THOMAS

Carmichael dug into his pocket and pulled out a silver dollar. "How 'bout I throw this up in the air and when it hits the ground, we both draw?"

"Okay."

Carmichael threw the coin as far up as he could and moved his right hand down by the butt of his pistol. The shiny coin spun up in the air and started downward. When it landed, Carmichael went to jerk his pistol out, but he heard what seemed like two shots and both cans went flying up in the air.

"What the...?" he muttered as he slowly swiveled his head toward Jess, who smiled and cocked his head slightly.

"Did that satisfy your curiosity?" he asked.

"Did you draw before the coin landed?"

"No."

"Then, how the hell did you do that?"

"I drew my gun and fired two shots."

Carmichael shook his head. "But it sounded more like one shot."

"I know."

"All right, I gotta see this for myself," he said as he holstered his pistol and walked around to Jess's right side. "Okay, now do that again."

"You gonna flip another coin?" he asked. Carmichael pulled out another silver dollar and flipped it into the air.

His eyes dropped to Jess's gun and what he saw next was something he would never forget.

In a blurring motion, Jess slicked his gun out, fired two shots that seemed as one and then fanned a third shot that caught the coin mid-air. Carmichael jerked his head toward the cans and saw them falling back to the ground, followed by the coin.

"I saw it, but I don't believe it," he muttered.

He walked out to the cans and found the coin on the ground. He picked it up and looked at the notch in it. He walked back to Jess as he was replacing his spent shells in his pistol. He showed the coin to Jess.

"I'm gonna keep this as my good luck charm," said Carmichael. "I guess not challenging you was the luckiest day in my miserable life."

Jess holstered his pistol and grinned at him. "Make me a promise," said Jess.

"What?"

"What you just saw, you didn't see."

"You have my word on it," said Carmichael chuckling. "Besides, who would believe me anyway?"

They climbed up in the saddle and started heading along the trail again. Carmichael kept glancing at Jess's pistol and shaking his head.

CHAPTER THIRTY-THREE

When Jess and Carmichael started along the trail heading into Hades, they both stopped when they saw the sign. It was nailed to a pole that was in the ground. The sign said: Welcome to Williamstown.

Carmichael patted Jess on the shoulder. "Damn if they didn't name the town after you," he laughed.

"I never would have thought they'd do that," Jess said as he stared at the sign.

The two continued along the rocky trail and when they caught the first glimpse of the town, they both stopped and leaned back in the saddle. All the buildings were painted white except for one building, the saloon, still the original dark red. The name above the door was painted in bold white letters. It read: Williamstown Saloon.

"I guess you're even more famous now," chuckled Carmichael. "Looks like I'll be living in your town."

"I've never really thought of myself as famous," Jess muttered to himself as he looked at all the buildings. He smiled when he saw some men constructing a few new homes. "But it looks like the town is finally getting its life back."

They rode to the livery and stabled their horses. They were carrying their things to the saloon when the mayor and two councilmen approached them. The mayor stuck his hand out, but Jess's hands were full so he simply nodded at him.

"I see you've been busy," Jess told him as he looked around the town.

"We sure have," said the mayor. "We went to Chilton and got the white paint and painted every building except for the saloon. All the trails leading in and out of town are cleared and new signs erected at all of them. I suppose you saw the new name for the town?"

"I did, and thank you," said Jess. "You didn't have to name it after me though."

"Any name is better than Hades or Hell, and besides, if it weren't for you and Mr. Carmichael, we might have all ended up in the local cemetery."

Carmichael noticed two women planting flowers in front of a few homes. "The flowers look nice."

"Oh, that was my daughter Pearl's idea," said the mayor. "She thought it would make the town seem friendlier."

Carmichael swallowed hard and looked nervously at the mayor. "Pearl is your daughter?" he asked.

"Yes and she's done nothing but talk about you since you left," he replied. "Don't you worry none. Any man who has the kind of courage you two have is surely a man I'd love to have as a son-in-law."

"Thank you, sir," said Carmichael as Pearl walked out of one of the houses where the flowers were being planted. She headed straight for them and everyone turned to watch her. She walked straight up to Carmichael and kissed him on his cheek.

"I see you came back to me," she said playfully.

"Only a bullet would have stopped me."

"Did you finally catch up with the rest of those horrible men?"

"We did," said Carmichael. "They won't be bothering anyone else ever again."

"Good," she said. "Now, you go and get cleaned up, settled in and then we can discuss the wedding." Carmichael's mouth fell open, but no words came out.

Jess elbowed him. "What? Nothing to say?" he asked. Carmichael just stood there with his mouth open, looking back and forth between the mayor and Pearl.

"Daddy has nothing to say about this," she told him. "And I expect you to build me a house for us to live in before we start talking about children."

"I…I don't know exactly what to say," stammered Carmichael. "I was coming back to court you and then maybe ask you to marry me."

Pearl put her hands on her hips and pouted. "Maybe?" she asked with her eyes narrowed and her lips tightened.

"Well, no…I mean…I would have eventually asked you to marry me, but I figured we'd have to spend some time together first to see if we're fitted for one another," he said nervously.

"Eventually?" she demanded, as everyone watched Carmichael squirming like a worm being hunted by a bunch of hungry crows.

The mayor finally stepped in to help. "Now dear, let the man get settled in and then you two can talk about the future," he said.

Pearl huffed and then smiled. "I'll expect you at five for supper at our house, Mr. Jason Carmichael," she said before turning around and heading back to the house.

"Wow," said Carmichael as relief washed over him. "Is she always like that?"

The mayor nodded and laughed. "She's been like that since my wife passed on. She took over the household and she doesn't dillydally about…well…anything, as you plainly saw."

"I guess not," said a much more comfortable Carmichael.

The mayor turned to Jess. "Mr. Williams, we still have some of the money you gave us. We paid men to clear all the trails and do all the painting. I'll gladly give you what's left, that is, unless you'd like to have your name on a new schoolhouse?"

Jess was about to respond when Carmichael interrupted him. "I'll pay for a new schoolhouse," he offered.

The mayor turned back to Carmichael. "You will?" he asked.

"Yes, and anything else the town needs," Carmichael said grinning.

"You can afford that?" asked the mayor skeptically.

"I can," boasted Carmichael. "I recently came into some extra money and since I'm making this my new home, I might as well invest in it."

"All right, but you'd better save some for the wedding because she's been talking about how nice she wants it to be," cautioned the mayor. "She's going to invite everyone in town, not that it's a lot of people after the Ropers murdered so many."

"Don't worry," chuckled Jess. "He can afford it now."

"Well then, I'll see the both of you at supper at my house later," said the mayor as he and the two councilmen walked away.

Jess turned to Carmichael, who was looking over at Pearl standing on the front porch of the house. "You sure you can handle her?" he asked.

"I think she'll be a bit more work than dealing with the Roper gang, but yeah, she's worth it," he said as they headed for the saloon to drop off their things.

CHAPTER THIRTY-FOUR

The wedding happened four days later in the middle of Main Street. It was a grand celebration with food and drink and even toys for the children in town. Jess tried to pay for some of it, but Carmichael wouldn't hear a word of it. The party lasted all day long and everyone in town was happy for the first time in a long while.

The mayor opened the jail again and swore Carmichael in as the new town marshal. The bank in town was more than happy to handle the money Carmichael had. Jess had them wire most of his share of the bounty to his bank in Black Creek, Kansas. The celebration was winding down as the sun headed toward the western skyline. Jess was standing at the bar in the saloon when someone tapped him on the shoulder. It was the same old man who had carried his two cut-down shotguns into the saloon after the gun battle between him and Carmichael and the Roper gang.

"What do you want?" Jess asked him.

"Some good whiskey if you can spare some," he said as he looked at the bottle on the bar. Jess handed him the bottle, which was almost full.

The man grinned from ear to ear. "Thanks, Mr. Williams," he said. "And the good stuff too." He took the bottle and a glass over to a table and sat down.

Jess turned back to the barkeep. "What's the story on the old man?" he asked.

"Oh, that's a long one," sighed Archer. "He used to be one of the best at skinning a hog leg out from leather. He was wanted for a time, but then he turned honest and even pinned on a badge for a bit. Now he's just old and living in my shed out back. He sweeps the place out and empties the spittoons at night for a meal and some whiskey."

"Sounds a bit like your story," Jess told Archer with a witty smile.

"Huh?"

"You didn't think I knew?"

"Knew what?"

"That you were wanted by the law some years back and here you are, owner of a saloon and making an honest living."

"How'd you know about that?"

"I remember seeing an old wanted poster with your face on it a few years ago."

"Then why didn't you try to collect on it?"

"You weren't wanted dead or alive and besides, you look like you're an honest businessman now, so you can take your left hand off that sawed-off I know you keep below the bar," Jess told him as he raised his eyebrows and grinned.

Archer's face flushed with embarrassment as he brought his hand up. "Sorry. Old habits die hard, I guess," he said. "And thanks."

"You're welcome. So, why did you leave the saloon painted red?"

"I decided we all needed to remember what happened here. We can't forget all the good folks who lost their lives to those killers for no good reason."

"I suppose maybe that's a good thing," admitted Jess as he placed a five-dollar gold piece on top of the bar.

Jess went to his room upstairs and cleaned and oiled all his weapons. He looked at the wanted posters he had in his pocket. He had three and he looked them over thoroughly, burning the images of the men into his brain. He fell off to sleep with the chair under the door handle and his pistol on his lap as always.

In the morning, he had breakfast in a café on Main Street. He was sipping hot coffee when Carmichael walked in wearing a wide smile on his face and a shiny new badge on his shirt. Everyone in the place acknowledged him. A few men even shook his hand as he made his way to the back table. He finally sat down across from Jess.

"Did the rest of the night go as well as the party?" Jess asked.

"It sure did." He chuckled as he took his hat off. "She's one feisty woman, but I love her."

"You've made a huge change in your life," Jess told him. "Not long ago, you found me with vengeance in your heart and wanting to kill me. Now, you're a happy man with a new bride, a new job and plenty of money to live on."

"I would have never thought this would happen to the likes of me. And, I owe it all to the man I was planning on killing. Seems kind of strange the way things turned out."

"Give yourself some credit. You made the right decisions along the way that got you here."

ROBERT J. THOMAS

"Especially the decision not to challenge you to a gunfight," he admitted. "So, what now for you? Care to stay in town? I'll even have a house built for you if you want to settle down."

Jess shook his head and grinned. "Naw, I have a wanted man to hunt," he said.

"I knew you'd say that, which is why I brought you these," he said as he pulled some wanted posters out of his pocket and unfolded them. Jess looked them over and folded them back up, putting them in his front pocket with the others he had.

"Thanks, Marshal," he said. "Tell me, what made you decide to pin that badge on?"

"Well, the position was open and I figured I was the best person in town for the job," he said proudly.

"She told you to do it, didn't she?"

"Yeah, she said I needed to have a job no matter how much money I had," he admitted reluctantly.

"Well, you are the best man in town for the job. You don't run from a fight. I know that to be a fact."

"When are you leaving?"

"As soon as I get my things over at the saloon and buy some supplies."

"Make sure you stop and say goodbye to Pearl."

"I will," Jess said as they both stood up and shook hands. "It was really good working with you."

"The pleasure was all mine," proclaimed Carmichael. "I don't suppose I need to tell you that you're welcome back here any time you want to visit."

"Thanks," said Jess as he walked out of the café. Carmichael watched him go out the door and turn toward the saloon. The waitress walked over to him.

"Marshal, would you like something to eat?"

"Well, I already had breakfast, but what the heck, I could go for a piece of apple pie and some coffee to go with it," he said as he sat back down.

Jess collected his things from the room above the saloon. He headed for the livery and saddled his horses. He walked them over to the general store, purchased some things and packed them into his saddlebags. When he finished, he saw Pearl standing on the front porch of her house and he walked his horses over to her.

"You're leaving already?" she asked.

"Yeah, I've stayed too long already." She walked down the steps and gave him a big hug.

"Thank you so much for bringing him back to me alive."

"He's a good man. You take care of him and he'll take care of you."

"I will, and thanks again for everything," she said as she let go of him.

He climbed up in the saddle and headed north out of town. When he reached the new town sign, he turned Gray around to look at it. He smiled as he gazed back at the town. It looked completely different now. He turned Gray back around and put him into a slow gallop when he hit the flatland. The smile slowly changed to a determined look as he thought about the next man he would hunt.

The End

READ THE ENTIRE SERIES OF JESS WILLIAMS WESTERNS

(LISTED IN ORDER)

BODY COUNT
HUNT DOWN
FROM THE GRAVE
BLACK RAVEN
THE BOUNTY HUNTERS
TO HELL AND BACK
MACHETE
STREETS OF LAREDO
RIDE OF REVENGE
COLD JUSTICE
GOD'S GUN
DARK CLOUD
REDEMPTION
TROUBLE IN NAVARRO
BLACK HEART
THE JOURNEY
THE TRANSPORT
PAINTED LADIES
RANGE WAR
CROSSROADS
DEATH BY LEAD
DUNDEE
A CHRISTMAS MIRACLE
OLD GUNS
WILD CAT
HADES
FOOL'S GOLD
DEVIL'S DUE

COMING SOON: THE NEXT BOOK IN THE JESS WILLIAMS WESTERN SERIES

Also look for *Wanted, A Western Story Collection* by Robert J. Thomas and six other western authors. *The Shepherd* is a short story by Robert J. Thomas in the collection featuring Jess Williams.

Made in the USA
Monee, IL
03 March 2020

22651031R00138